Anonymous

The Catholic School Book

containing easy and familiar lessons for the instruction of youth, of both sexes, in

the English language and the paths of true religion and virtue

Anonymous

The Catholic School Book
containing easy and familiar lessons for the instruction of youth, of both sexes, in the English language and the paths of true religion and virtue

ISBN/EAN: 9783337391959

Printed in Europe, USA, Canada, Australia, Japan

Cover: Foto ©Andreas Hilbeck / pixelio.de

More available books at **www.hansebooks.com**

THE CATHOLIC
SCHOOL BOOK,

CONTAINING

EASY AND FAMILIAR LESSONS

FOR THE

INSTRUCTION OF YOUTH,

OF BOTH SEXES,

IN THE ENGLISH LANGUAGE

AND THE

PATHS OF TRUE RELIGION AND VIRTUE.

ELEVENTH MONTREAL EDITION, CORRECTED.

PART I.

Tables of Words, of one, two, three, four, five, six and seven syllables ; also Easy Reading Lessons taken from the Holy Scriptures, with a Moral to each Lesson.

PART II.

Lessons on the End for which Man was created ; on what it is to be a Christian ; on the necessity of being virtuous in the time of Youth ; on Prayer and Instruction ; on the Fear and Love of God ; on the Love of Parents, &c. ; on the Vices of Swearing and Lying, &c., &c.

PART III.

The Principal Festivals of the Church expounded. Necessary Rules for a Christian to follow. Prayers to be used on different occasions ; and a Summary of the Christian Doctrine.

MONTREAL.

FOR SALE AT THE BOOKSTORES.

1862.

THE SECOND LONDON EDITION.

———o———

THE rapid sale which the first edition of this book experienced, the whole impression having been sold in ten months, and the high encomiums which have been passed upon it by the most eminent of the Clergy, induces the Editor to offer a second to the patronage of the Catholic public, which he has enlarged, and he trusts, in some measure, improved. The spelling lessons will, on examination, be found better arranged, and some hundred words have been added to those which are similar in sound and different in spelling and sense.

In the second part two chapters are introduced, on the Devotion due to the Blessed Virgin, and to our Guardian-angel and Patron Saint.

Objections have been made to this work, because it does not contain some grammatical exercises; and also that the spelling lessons are not sufficiently prolix. To the first, the Editor begs to observe, that he never found such exercises to be of any service to children at the age when they use this book; and when they arrive at the proper period to study grammar, it is better for them to have a separate work on the subject, many of which are to be had. To the second it may be observed, that most of the reading lessons in the first part being divided into syllables by hyphens, they must be considered as adapted to the purpose of spelling as well as of reading. The editor's chief aim, in compiling this work, was to implant the seeds of Virtue and True Religion in the minds of the rising generation, at the time of imparting to them the knowledge of letters; convinced, as he is, that nothing is so necessary to insure the happiness of mankind, as to train up a child in the way he should go, for when he is old he will not depart from it. If the divine precepts of a Christian life, and the necessary means of fulfilling them, are but firmly rooted in the minds of youth of both sexes, they will not fail to become virtuous ornaments of the Catholic Church, worthy members of society here, and happy citizens of heaven hereafter. The following pages may be found useful in attaining these desirable blessings is the sincere and fervent prayer of.

W. E. ANDREWS.

CATHOLIC SCHOOL BOOK.

THE ALPHABET.

ROMAN.

A B C D E F G H I J
K L M N O P Q R S T U
V W X Y Z

a b c d e f g h i j k l m n o p
q r s t u v w x y z

ITALIC.

A B C D E F G H I J K
L M N O P Q R S T U V
W X Y Z

a b c d e f g h i j k l m n o p
q r s t u v w x y z

THE ALPHABET CROSSED.

A D G K M L C B J R O
E T F N Q V P W Y I S
H U Z X

a k j v o e n q h p i d g l r t m
b x c f u w z s

VOWELS.

a   e   i   o   u   y

CONSONANTS.

b c d f g h j k l m n p q r s t v w x z

DOUBLE AND TREBLE LETTERS.

ff   fi   fl   ffi   ffl

TABLE I.

LESSON I.					LESSON II.				
ba	ce	di	fo	ku	ab	ib	oc	um	eb
ka	fe	ci	do	bu	im	af	ud	ob	ec
fo	de	ko	bi	ca	if	om	ub	ac	ed
du	ke	be	co	fi	od	ef	ib	uc	ad
cu	da	bo	fu	ki	uf	am	of	em	ec

LESSON III.					LESSON IV.				
ma	ri	no	ti	se	en	at	in	an	os
ta	su	re	mu	ni	ax	es	ix	or	un
ru	mi	to	sa	ne	it	ur	ex	on	ar
te	si	me	na	ro	ox	ut	as	er	in
ra	tu	mo	nu	so	et	is	us	an	ot

LESSON V.				LESSON VI.			
bla	ple	flo	clu	bra	pre	tro	cru
fli	ble	cla	plu	tri	bre	cra	pru
cle	fla	pli	blo	cre	tra	pri	bro
pla	fle	bli	clo	pra	tre	bri	cro

LESSON VII.				
fra	fru	fri	fro	fre
phra	phru	phri	phro	phre

TABLE II.

LESSON I. *Words of three Letters.*

All	try	and	are	bed	yet	don	for	sup	the
you	her	not	thy	two	off	men	sin	low	tic
pod	fun	hap	pig	dun	nag	sod	kid	red	mud
tun	fag	nip	gun	hod	did	cud	wed	sip	rod
bee	oil	tea	dot	nut	act	sea	bun	fit	mad

LESSON II. *Words of four Letters.*

Cake	hare	mark	make	cart	dart
bark	span	fall	dark	wake	tall
mart	knot	mare	pass	writ	clod
wink	lock	shut	fail	such	dock
boil	hook	blot	them	sand	drub

LESSON III.

Mope	bail	sake	book	mace	pail
look	mock	pace	band	nail	hope
land	race	that	term	glut	knit
name	wise	your	gave	then	whom
bare	what	bird	mind	have	walk
beau	suit	hail	grim	knob	smut

LESSON IV. *Words of five Letters.*

Faith	reign	pease	cause	chief	fruit
daunt	stood	brawl	pause	couch	joint
might	voice	teach	vouch	thief	moist
knack	eight	bench	small	brass	track
faint	quick	stack	knead	poach	drawn
saith	craft	frame	pouch	taste	clock
shaft	check	right	pride	guild	crown

TABLE III.

LESSON I. *Names of Birds, Beasts, &c.*

Cat	dog	cow	calf	hog	horse
mare	colt	bear	crane	crow	dove
cock	hen	hawk	kite	flea	frog
ant	snipe	bug	lark	owl	rook

LESSON II. *Terms used at Play, &c.*

Ball	bat	skip	cards	dice	chuck
gig	leap	jump	throw	kite	spin
top	trap	taw	whip	lose	win

LESSON III. *Apparel.*

Cap	hap	coif	hood	coat	cloak
frock	fan	gown	gloves	lace	muff
hoop	knot	scarf	stays	shoes	clogs
shirt	shift	cloth	stuff	plush	silk

LESSON IV. *Eatables.*

Ale	beer	tea	wine	bread	cheese
crust	buns	crumb	cakes	pies	tarts
beef	lamb	pork	veal	fish	flesh
beans	peas	milk	cream	curds	whey

LESSON V. *Trees, Plants, Fruits, &c.*

Ash	hay	beech	birch	box	elm
fir	lime	oak	pine	vine	yew
broom	hemp	flax	fern	grass	herbs
hops	reeds	rose	rue	sage	shrub
oats	rye	wheat	crabs	figs	nuts
plums	pears	grapes	leaf	roots	trees

LESSON VI. *Titles and Names.*

King	duke	peer	wife	aunt	Mark
queen	earl	knight	child	niece	Luke
prince	lord	page	son	bride	John

LESSON VII. *Number, Weights, &c.*

One	five	nine	inch	drop	drachm
two	six	ten	foot	dram	ounce
three	seven	once	ell	pint	pound
four	eight	twice	yard	quart	score

LESSON VIII. *Parts of the Body.*

Head	hair	face	eyes	nose	mouth
scull	brain	tongue	lips	teeth	chin
arms	hands	cheeks	throat	breast	ears
back	bones	thumb	shins	fist	wrist
toes	nails	knees	ribs	legs	feet

LESSON IX. *The World.*

Sun	east	cape	clay	brook	frost
moon	west	rock	dirt	pool	snow
stars	north	land	bank	pond	mist
air	south	hill	sand	rain	dew
wind	earth	isles	chalk	hail	ice

LESSON X. *Things belonging to a House.*

Cup	door	chest	stool	quilt	thatch
cock	box	chair	coach	slate	mug
bench	brush	plate	bed	tiles	key
pot	stone	broom	spoon	lock	spit
paint	lime	fork	latch	jack	stairs
brick	knife	bolt	grate	glass	sheet

TABLE IV.

Easy Lessons of One Syllable, by which a child will sooner know both the Sound and use of e final.

Al	ale	dot	dote	mod	mode	rud	rude
ar	are	Fam	fame	mol	mole	Sal	sale
at	ate	fan	fane	mop	mope	sam	same
Bab	babe	far	fare	mor	more	sid	side
bal	bale	fat	fate	Nam	name	sin	sine
ban	bane	fil	file	nap	nape	sit	site
bar	bare	fin	fine	nil	nile	sol	sole
bas	base	for	fore	nod	node	sur	sure
bid	bide	Gal	gale	nor	nore	Tal	tale
bil	bile	gam	game	not	note	tam	tame
bit	bite	gap	gape	Od	ode	tap	tape
Can	cane	gat	gate	or	ore	tar	tare
cam	came	gor	gore	Pan	pane	tid	tide
car	care	Hal	hale	pat	pate	til	tile
cap	cape	hat	hate	pin	pine	tim	time
col	cole	her	here	pol	pole	tin	tine
cop	cope	hid	hide	por	pore	ton	tone
cor	core	hop	hope	pil	pile	top	tope
Dal	dale	Kin	kine	Rat	rate	tub	tube
dam	dame	kit	kite	rid	ride	tun	tune
dan	dane	Lad	lade	rip	ripe	Val	vale
dar	dare	Mad	made	rit	rite	van	vane
dat	date	man	mane	rob	robe	vil	vile
din	dine	mar	mare	rod	rode	vot	vote
dol	dole	mat	mate	rop	rope	Wad	wade
dom	dome	mil	mile	rot	rote	win	wine

Do all that is just, and God will love you. Call on Him, and He will help you. Seek the Lord, and you will find Him.

I will pray to the Lord all the day long.

TABLE V.

Lessons of One Syllable.

Who made you and gave you life ? God, who made the world and all things in it.

And was there a time when there was not a God ? No ; there was no time when God was not.

Who is God ? He, my child, who made the world ; made you, and gave you life, and your soul.

He, the same who made the sun, the moon, the stars, the birds that fly in the air, the fish that swim in the sea, the beasts that walk and feed in the fields ; in a word, all the things which you see, and which give you joy.

Did God make the world all at once ? No. He made it in the space of six days. Could he not have made it at once ? Yes, if such had been his will.

What ought you to do at the sight and use of things which God hath made? I ought to raise up my mind and heart to Him, and to praise him.

Why do we name him by that word or name of God ? What doth that name mean ? This is He, my child, the Great One, the Good One, and the Wise One, God. Of whom all things, as it were, cry out unto us with one voice : Know ye, Men, that the Lord He is God, it is he that hath made us.

Raise up then your mind, your heart, and your voice to him, and say ; O God, Thou art great, and good, and wise : Thou art the one God and Lord of all things.

All men and all things that have been made, and that now are, were made by God ; but God was not made.

For there was a time when there was no man, nor bird, nor fish ; but there was not a time when there was no God, or when God was not.

He is the Lord and God of all men, and things that have been, and that are, and that will be.— All are made by him, and all live and move by Him. God is, and was, and will be.

The eye of God is on all men. I will mind the way of the Lord, my God, that I may not sin. If sin be in us we are in a bad way. Let us go out of it, as it is not good for us to be in it.

In God do I put my joy, and to Him will I cry all day. Keep me, O Lord, from such as love not thy law, and walk not in thy ways. I see thy way, O God, and I joy in it.

TABLE VI.

Words of Two Syllables, accented on the first.

[The single accent (') denotes the right emphasis of the syllables and the double accent (") shews that the following consonant is to be pronounced double; thus, ba"nish is pronounced bannish.]

Ab' ba	an vil	bor row	cam phire
Ab bot	ar bor	boun ty	can cel
ab bess	arch er	brack et	can cer
ab bey	arc tic	brand isb	can did
ab ject	ar dent	bra zen	can dour
ac cent	art ful	brit tle	can vass
a' cid	art ist	bro ker	cap tive
a cre	as pect	bru mal	car bine
ac tive	at las	buck ler	car cass
ac tor	au dit	buck ram	car go
a" dage	a zure	bud get	car nage
ad der	Bai liff	bulb ous	cart ridge
ad verse	ba" lance	bul wark	carv ing
a gent	baf fle	bun gler	cas tle
ail ing	bal lot	bur then	can dle
am ble	bane ful	bur den	ca" vern
am bush	bank er	bur gess	cause way
am ple	ba" nish	bur nish	caus tic
an chor	barb ed	but ter	ce rate
an gel	bar ren	but tress	ceil ing
an gle	ba sis	Ca' ble	chair man
an guish	bea con	cal lous	cha" lice
an nals	bi as	cal low	chal lenge
an them	bil low	ca" lid	chan cel
cha os	co gent	cos tive	de ist
cha" pel	co'n age	co" vert	de" luge

chap let	com pact	cur rent	drea ry
char ter	com pass	cus tom	driz zle
chat tels	com plex	cut ler	dro psy
cheer ful	com rade	cy" nic	dro ver
cheer less	con cave	cy press	drow sy
che" rish	con cord	Dab ble	drug gist
chief tain	con course	dain ty	duc tile
chi" sel	con flict	da" mage	du el
cho rus	con flux	da" mask	duke dom
chris ten	con gress	dan ger	Ea ger
chur lish	con quest	dar nel	ea gle
chy" mist	con serve	das tard	ear less
ci pher	con sort	dea con	ear nest
cir cle	con strue	debt or	earth en
cir cuit	con tact	de cent	east ward
cis tern	con trive	des pot	e" cho
ci" tron	con vent	de" sert	e dict
ci" vil	con vex	dic tate	ef fort
claim ant	cor net	di et	e gress
cla" mour	cor nice	di' git	em blem
clas sic	cor sair	dis cord	em pire
clea ver	co" vet	dis mal	en dive
cle" mant	cou" rage	dis tick	en gine
cli mate	count ess	dis trict	eu trails
cli ent	coun try	dole ful	en vy
clus ter	coun ty	do" lour	e pic
cof fer	cre" dit	dol phin	e qual
col league	crim son	do nor	e ra
col lege	cri sis	dor mant	es sence
co" lumn	cri" tic	do tage	e" tic
com bat	crys tal	do" zen	eu rope
co" met	cul ture	dra ma	ex ile
com ment	cu rate	dra per	ex it

ex tant	fo'' rage	gen tle	hea vy
Fa'' bric	fo'' reign	ges ture	heart felt
fa ble	for feit	ghast ly	hea then
fac tor	forg er	gher kin	hec tor
faith ful	for mal	gid dy	head less
fa'' mish	for tress	glit ter	hei nous
fa mous	fos ter	glut ton	hei fer
fan cy	foun der	gos pel	hel met
fa'' thom	frac ture	go'' thic	hem lock
fa vour	fra grant	go'' vern	her bal
flo'' rid	frag ment	gram mar	her mit
fee ble	frail ty	gran deur	he ro
fe'' lon	fran tic	grap ple	higg ler
fer tile	fren zy	grate ful	hire ling
fer vour	fri'' gid	gra tis	hi'' ther
fi bre	fro'' lic	gra ver	hoa ry
fic kle	fron tier	gross ness	ho'' mage
fi'' gure	fru gal	gro'' vel	ho'' nest
fi nal	fruit less	guid ance	ho'' nour
fi nis	frus trate	guil ty	hor ror
fi nite	fur nish	Ha'' bit	hos tage
fla grant	fur nace	hack ney	hos tile
flat ter	fur row	ham per	ho'' ver
fla vour	fu tile	hand cuff	hum ble
fledg ed	fu ture	hand some	hu mid
fleet ness	Ga'' mut	har row	hu mour
flex ure	gab ble	har vest	hys sop
flo'' rist	gar gle	hat chet	I dle
flu id	gar ment	ha ven	ill ness
flu ent	gar nish	haugh ty	i'' mage
flut ter	gau dy	ha'' voc	im port
fod der	gan grene	hawk er	im pulse
foi ble	guag ing	ha'' zard	in come

in dex	la tent	mar ble	mo" ral
in gress	lat tice	mar gin	mor tar
in let	la" vish	mar shal	mort gage
in jure	law yer	mar tyr	mo tive
in mate	le gal	mar vel	mot ley
in quest	le" gate	mas sy	mot to
in road	le gend	match less	mourn ful
in sect	lei sure	mat tress	mun dane
in sight	le" vel	mau gre	mur mur
in stance	li bel	max im	mus cle
in stinct	li cense	may or	myr tle
irk some	lim ner	mea" dow	muz zle
isl and	lim pid	mea gre	Na tive
isth mus	lin guist	me" dal	na ture
is sue	li' quor	me" nace	na vy
i tem	li" vid	men tal	nee dy
Ja lap	lo cal	mer cer	ner vous
joint ture	lo" gic	me" rit	ne" ther
junc ture	loy al	mes sage	neu' ter
jun to	lu cid	me ter	nig gard
Ken nel	lu cre	mid night	ni tre
ker sey	lug gage	migh ty	no ble
kid der	lus ter	min gle	noi some
king dom	ly ric	mi nor	non age
kna vish	Mag net	mir ror	non plus
kit chen	main ed	mis chief	nos trum
knuc kle	ma" lice	mi tre	no" ve
La' bel	mam mon	mo" del	no vice
la bent	ma" nage	mo" dern	nou" rish
la bour	man date	mod est	nui sance
lan cet	man gle	mo dish	nur ture
lan guid	ma" nor	mo ment	Oat meal
lan guish	man tle	mo" narch	ob long

o cean	pa" tron	port ly	pru dence
o dour	pau per	por trait	psal mist
of fal	pea sant	post age	psal ter
off spring	pe dant	pos ture	pur blind
o men	ped lar	po tent	pur port
op tic	pee vish	prac tice	pus tule
o ral	pe nal	prat tle	pu trid
ord nance	pe" nance	pre cept	Rab ble
or dure	pen sive	pre cinct	rab bit
or phan	pe" ril	pre" late	rai ment
os trich	pe" rish	pre" lude	ral ly
o val	pes ter	pre sure	ram part
o vert	pes tle	pri mate	ran cour
out rage	phan tom	pri or	ran dom
oys ter	phœ nix	pris tine	ran sack
Pack et	phi al	pri" vy	ran ter
pad dle	phy sic	pro" blem	ra" pid
pa gan	pil fer	pro" cess	ra" pine
pa" lace	pil grim	proc tor	rap ture
pal try	pin nace	pro" duct	rash ness
pam per	pi ous	pro" fit	ra" vage
pam phlet	pla" card	pro fer	rea son
pa" nic	plain tiff	pro" gress	re cent
pan cake	plat form	pro" ject	rec tor
pan nel	plu mage	pro" logue	re flux
par boil	plun der	pro noun	re" fuge
par ley	plu ral	pro" phet	re gal
par lour	poig nant	pros pect	re gent
pas sive	po" lish	pros trate	re" lict
pas tor	pom mel	pro" verb	re lish
pas ture	pom pous	pro" vince	rem nant
pa" tent	pon der	prow ess	ren der
pa thos	pon tiff	pru dent	rep tile

re" spite	scho" lar	sig net	spot less
re" vel	sci ence	sil van	spright ly
rhu barb	sci on	si" new	sprin kle
ri" gid	scrib ble	six ty	sqa" lid
ri ot	scrip ture	skil ful	squal ly
ri val	scru ple	skil led	squan der
ro guish	sculp tor	skir mish	sta ble
ro" sin	sculp ture	slaugh ter	stag nant
ros trum	se cret	slen der	, stam mer
roy al	sei zure	sloth ful	stand ard .
ru bric	self ish	slo" ven	stand ish
rug ged	se" nate	slum ber	state ly
rum ble	sen tence	smo" ther	sta" tue
rum mage	se quel	smug gler	sta" ture
ru mour	ser mon	so journ	sta" tute
rup ture	ser vile	so" lace	stea dy
ru ral	se" ver	so lar	steer age
rus tic	sew er	so lemn	ste" ril
Sa ble	sex ton	so" lid	ster ling
sa bre	shal low	sol vent	stern ly
sa cred	sham bles	son net	stew art
sad dle	shame ful	so" phist	stick ler
sal vage	shame less	sor did	stig ma
sam ple	shar per	sor rel	sti pend
san guine	shat ter	sor row	sto" mach
sap phire	shet ter	spar kle	sto ry
sar casm	she" riff	spat ter	stow age
saun ter	shrewd ly	spee dy	strag gle
scab bard	sbri" vel	spin dle	stran gle
scan dal	shud der	spi ral	strip ling
scep tic	scuf fle	spite ful	strug gle
scep tre	sic kle	splen did	stub born
sche" dule	sig nal	sport ing	stu dent

A 4

stub ble	Ta ber	tit tle	tu mour
stum ble	tab by	to ken	tu mult
stu pid	ta" lent	ton nage	tur bid
stu por	ta" lon	to" pic	tur gid
stur dy	tam per	tor ment	tur ret
sub tile	tap ster	tor pid	twin kle
sub t'e	tar get	tor rent	twit ter
sub urb	tar nish	tor rid	ty rant
suc cour	tart ness	tor toise	tym bal
sud den	taw dry	tor ture	Va cant
suf frage	tem per	to ward	va grant
suit or	tem pest	tow er	va" lid
sul len	tem ple	traf fic	val ley
sul ly	te" nant	tra" gic	va" lour
sul tan	ten der	trai tor	va" lue
sul try	ten don	tram ple	va" nish
sum mit	te" net	tran quil	va" pid
sum mer	ten ter	tran sit	va pour
sun dry	te" nure	tra vel	var nish
sup ple	ter race	tra" verse	vas sal
sur face	ter ror	trea cle	vel lum
sur feit	tes ter	trea son	ve" nom
sure ty	tex ture	trea tise	ver bal
sur name	thick et	tre mor	ver dict
sur plus	thirs ty	tre" pid	ver dure
swad dle	this tle	tres pass	ver nal
swar thy	thi" ther	tri bute	vers ed
swi" vel	tick et	tri fle	ver text
sym bol	til lage	tri" ple	ves pers
sy" nod	tim brel	troo per	ves sel
syn tax	ti" mid	tro phy	ves try
sy" ringe	tin kle	trow el	ves ture
sys tem	ti tle	tru ant	vi brate

rice roy	vol ley	wain scot	wor ry
vic tim	vo'' lume	wal let	wran gle
vic tor	vor tex	war ble	wrap per
vi'' gil	vouch er	war den	wres tle
vi'' gour	voy age	war fare	wrin kle
vil lage	vul gar	war rant	Yawn ing
vir tue	Um brage	war ren	yes ter
vi'' sage	um pire	weal thy	yeo men
vis count	up right	wea'' ther	youth ful
vis cous	up roar	weigh ty	Ze'' bra
vi'' sit	up shot	wel fare	zea lot
vi sor	ur gent	wher ry	zea lous
vi'' vid	Wa ger	wick et	ze nith
vo land	wad dle	wi'' dow	zig zag

TABLE VII.

Words of Two Syllables, accented on the last.

A base	ad dress	ap pease	as sign
a bat	ad duce	ap plause	as size
a bide	ad journ	ap ply	as suage
a bound	ad judge	ap point	as sume
ab solve	a dopt	ap proach	at tire
ab sorb	a dorn	ap prise	at tract
ab stain	ad vert	ap prove	a vail
ab struce	af firm	ar raign	a venge
ab surd	af fix	ar range	a vert
ac cede	al lege	ar rest	a verse
ac cess	al lude	as cribe	a void
ac cord	al lure	as sail	aug ment
ac crue	an nex	as pire	Be guile
ac cuse	an noy	as sault	be moan
ac quit	an nul	as sent	be nign
ad dict	ap pal	as sert	be queath

be reave	com prise	con tempt	de fense
be witch	com pute	con tend	de fend
bom bard	con ceal	con tent	de fer
bom bast	con cede	con trive	de fine
bri gade	con ceit	con trol	de form
bu reau	con ceive	con vene	de fraud
Ca det	con cise	con verge	de fray
ca jole	con clude	con vey	de fy
ca lash	con cur	con voke	de grade
cal cine	con dense	cor rect	de gree
ca nal	con dole	cor rode	de ject
ca noe	con duce	cor rupt	de lay
ca price	con fer	cor tes	de light
ca reen	con fess	De bar	de lude
ca reer	con fide	de base	de mand
ca ress	con firm	de bate	de mean
ca rouse	con form	de cant	de mise
car tel	con front	de cay	de mur
cas cade	con fuse	de cease	de note
ca shier	con fute	de ceit	de part
cha grin	con geal	de cide	de pend
chas tise	con join	de claim	de pict
co heir	con nect	de cline	de plore
com bine	con nive	de coy	de plume
com mand	con sign	de cry	de pose
com mit	con sist	de cree	de prave
com pare	con sol	de duce	de press
com pel	con spire	de duct	de prive
com pile	con strain	de face	de pute
com plete	con sult	de fame	de ride
com ply	con sume	de fault	de rive
com port	con tain	de fait	de scend
com pose	con temn	de fect	de scribe

de scry	dis guise	e lude	e vince
de sert	dis junct	em balm	ex act
de sign	dis may	em bark	ex alt
de sist	dis own	em broil	ex cel
de spair	dis patch	e merge	ex cess
de spoil	dis pel	e mit	ex cite
de spite	dis pense	en act	ex clude
de tach	dis play	en chant	ex empt
de tail	dis pute	en close	ex ert
de tain	dis pose	en croach	ex hale
de ter	dis robe	en dear	ex baust
de tect	dis sect	en dorse	ex hort
de test	dis sent	en dow	ex ist
de tract	dis solve	en dure	ex pand
de vise	dis tend	en force	ex pause
de void	dis tinct	en gage	ex pel
de volve	dis til	en gross	ex pend
de vote	dis tort	en hance	ex pense
de vout	dis use	en large	ex pert
dif fuse	di vert	en rage	ex pire
di gest	di vest	en rich	ex plain
di gress	di vine	en rol	ex plode
di late	di vorce	en sure	ex ploit
dis arm	dra goon	en tail	ex plore
dis buse	E clat	en tice	ex port
dis card	e clipse	en tire	ex tend
dis cern	ef face	en treat	ex tent
dis claim	ef fect	e quib	ex tinct
dis close	ef flux	e rase	ex tol
dis creet	e ject	e rect	ex tort
dis cuss	e lapse	es cape	ex treme
dis dain	e lect	e vade	ex trude
dis ease	e lope	e vent	ex ult

ex ude

Fa tigue

fi nance

fo ment

for bear

for go

for lorn

for swear

ful fil

Ga zette

gen teel

gre nade

Har poon

hu mane

huz za

Il lude

im bibe

im brue

im merse

im mure

im pair

im part

im peach

im pede

im pel

im pend

im plant

im plore

im ply

im pose

im press

im print

im pure

im pute

in case

in cense

in cite

in clude

in cur

in dent

in dict

in ert

in fect

in fer

in fest

in firm

in form

in fuse

in spect

in spire

in still

in tense

in tent

in ter

in trude

in veigh

in vert

in vest

in volve

in ure

Ja pan

je june

jo cose

ju ly

Main tain

mal treat

ma nure

ma rine

ma ture

mar que

mis deed

mis trust

mo lest

mo rose

my self

O bey

ob scene

ob scure

ob struct

ob trude

ob tuse

oc cult

oc cur

op pose

op press

or dain

out do

Pa rade

pa role

par take

per form

per mit

per plex

per sist

per spire

per tain

per vade

per verse

per vert

pe ruse

po lite

por tend

por tent

post pone

pre cede

pre cinct

pre cise

pre clude

pre dict

pre fer

pre mise

pre sage

pre scribe

pre side

pre sume

pre tence

pre tend

pre text

pre vail

pre vent

pro cure

pro fane

pro file

pro fess

pro found

pro lix

pro long

pro mote

pro pose

pro rogue

pro tect

pro test

pro tract	rè fute	rē plete	re venge
pro trude	re gain	re pose	re vere
pro vide	re gard	re press	re verse
pro voke	re gret	re prieve	re vert
pur loin	re hearse	re proach	re view
pur suit	re ject	re prove	re vile
pur vey	re lapse	re pulse	re vise
Qua drille	re late	re pute	re vive
Re bound	re lax	re quest	re voke
re build	re lease	re quite	re volt
re buke	re lent	re sent	rè volve
re cant	re lief	re serve	ro bust
re cede	re mark	re side	ro mance
re ceipt	re mind	ré sign	ro tund
re cess	re mit	re sist	Sa line
re claim	re morse	re sort	sa lute
re cline	re mote	re sound	sa voy
re close	re new	re source	scru toire
re coil	re cite	re spect	se cede
re count	re cluse	re spire	se clude
re course	re flux	re strain	se crete
re cruit	re cur	re sult	se cure
re deem	re fit	re sume	se date
re dound	re gale	re tail	se duce
re dress	re miss	re tain	se lect
re duce	re nown	re tard	se rene
re fer	re pair	re tire	se vere
re fine	re past	re tort	se tee
re flect	re peal	re tract	shal loon
re form	re peat	re treat	sha green
re frain	re pel	re trench	so ho
re fresh	re pent	re trieve	sin cere
re fund	re pine	re veal	spi net

sub due	sup press	trans form	un nerve
sub join	su preme	trans fuse	un kind
sub lime	sur charge	trans gress	un knit
sub mit	sur mise	trans late	un known
sub orn	sur mount	trans mit	un lace
sub scribe	sur pass	trans mute	un lade
sub side	sur round	trans pierce	un laid
sub sist	sur vey	trans pire	un latch
sub vert	sur vive	trans plant	un learn
suc ceed	sus pect	trans port	un less
suc cess	sus pend	trans pose	un like
suc cinct	sus pense	trans verse	un link
suf fice	sus pire	tre pan	un load
sug gest	sub merge	trus tee	un lock
su perb	Tra duce	Ver bose	un loose
su pine	tran sact	vouch safe	un make
sup plant	tran scend	Un couth	un mask
sup ply	tran scribe	un fold	un made
sup port	trans fer	u nite	un moor
sup pose	trans fix		

TABLE VIII.

Easy Lessons of Two and Three Syllables.

Lesson I.

Hear now, my child, what great works God did when He made the world. Though he could have made the world all at once, if such had been His will, yet He did not make it all at once. He made all things, and man, in the space of six days. Thus He shew-ed that He made it not by force, but by His own free will and choice.

On the first day God made the Hea-ven and the earth, or that which was to be the world. The earth had not then the form it now hath. There was not the sun, nor the moon, nor the stars. It was a mass or heap, with no form or shape. And it was void, for there were no beasts, nor trees, nor birds, nor a-ny thing in it.

Nor was there a ny thing out of which God made the world. He is of such might, He is so great and

wise, that He did not need any help.   There was no light;
it was quite dark.   God then said, *Be light made, and
light was made.*

Not, my child, that God spoke such words as we may
speak them, for God is not as we are.   He hath not a
bo-dy as we have, so as He can be seen by us.   *No man
hath seen God at any time, nor can see him.*   He is a pure
spi-rit, the same as your own soul, a spi-rit which cannot be seen with mor-tal eyes.

Yet God knows and sees all things, and can do all things.
And He doth what He pleas-es by His will: His will was
and is as his word: hence, as soon as he would have a thing
be made or done, so soon was it made or done.

Thus it was His will there should be light, and there was
light; and a like of all o-ther things that were made.   And
God saw the light that it was good, and He call-ed the light
Day, and the dark-ness Night.

Now then, my child, and at all times when you look at, or
think on, the works of God, raise up your mind and heart to
that great and good God ; pray to Him and say : O God !
Thou art great and good and wise in all Thy works.   Bless
the Lord, all the works of the Lord.   Thou art my God,
by Thee I have been made, and by Thee I now live.

I pray Thee, O God, dart forth a ray of the light of Thy
grace on my mind and heart, that I may know Thee : then
will I a-dore Thee, I will praise Thee, I will love Thee,
and I will serve Thee by day and by night. ˙

LESSON II.

God makes the World and Man.

On the se-cond day, God made that part of the Hea-ven
which we call the Sky and the Air.   On the third day, He
set-tled the wa-ter in one place, and it was call-ed the Sea,
and the dry land He call-ed the Earth, then He made the
Herbs, Trees, and Plants, of all sorts, spring out of the
earth.

On the fourth day, God said, Be there lights to shine and
to give light by day and by night.   And God made

B

two great lights : the Sun, to rule or give light by day ; and the Moon and Stars, to rule or give light by night.

On the fifth day God made the Fish-es of the sea, and the Birds of the air. On the sixth day, He brought forth from the earth the Beasts, all that creep on the earth in its kind.

When God had made all these things, He then made Man, and He gave him rule over the Fish-es of the sea, the Fowls of the air, the Beasts, and over the whole earth.

Though Man was the last of the works which God made, yet he is the first in rank, and the most perfect of all the things in this world. Now, God form-ed the bo-dy of Man out of the slime of the earth ; then He breath-ed in-to it the breath of life.

By this breath of life is meant not only that by which Man breathes, and lives, and moves, as the beasts and birds do, but by it also is meant that which beasts have not, that is, a spirit, the Soul.

This is quite dis-tinct from the body, and by this Man knows God, who made him : he can think on Him, and love Him ; he can also think on, judge, and talk of things ; and by it he hath a will to do, or not to do, this or that thing, as he may choose or like best.

God did not take nor form this part of Man, or his soul, from the earth, as He did the bo-dy, but it came from God him-self, and God him-self in-fus-ed it in-to him. It is in this that Man is the most per-fect of all the works of God, be-cause by that Man is like to God.

Thus God made Man like to him-self, that Man might in this life know him (his God and his Lord, his be-gin-ning and end,) and love Him, and serve Him ; and by so do-ing see Him, and live with Him, and en-joy Him after this life, in Hea-ven.

MORAL.

Thus you see, my child, God hath made us much a-bove the beasts. He hath taught us more than the Beasts of the earth, and made us wis-er than the Birds of the air. Now, my child, He who hath been the cause of these and such great things for the use of Man, must have a great love for him.

Hence, we can-not too much love Him for all the love He shews us. Use then the things of the World as the kind gifts of the good God. When you use them, or they give you joy, raise up your mind and heart to praise and thank Him.

Say at least in your mind, and with your heart, How great art Thou, O God! how wise, and how good in all Thy works. Bless the Lord, all the works of the Lord; Sun, Moon, and Stars, Beasts of the field, Birds of the air, Fish-es of the sea, bless the Lord; ye sons of Men, bless the Lord; and thou, my soul, for whom the Lord hath done such great things, bless the Lord.

LESSON III.

God makes Eve. The sin of A-dam and Eve.
Genesis ii. 3.

God gave the first man whom he made, the name of A-dam, for that he had been made of the slime of the earth, God plac-ed him in the Garden of Pa-ra-dise, to work, and to keep it. God then brought to A-dam the Beasts of the earth, and the fowls of the air, or caus-ed them to come to him, that he might see them; and by what name he called them, the same is the name of each of them.

God cast A-dam into a deep sleep, and whilst he was a-sleep, God took a rib from his side, and he made it into a wo-man. He then brought her to A dam, and when A-dam saw her, he said: This is now bone of my bone, and flesh of my flesh, she shall be call-ed Woman, for that she is ta-ken out of Man. And she was al-so call-ed Eve, that is, the mo-ther of all men and wo-men that were thence to be born and to live.

There was in the midst of the gar-den, a tree. God bade A-dam and Eve not to eat, nor to touch, the fruit of it. He told them that if they did they should die. But Eve be-ing tempt-ed by the De-vil, in the form of a ser-pent, took of the fruit, and did eat; she then gave it to A-dam, and he ate of it. As soon as they had eat-en it, God call-ed to A-dam, and said, Where are thou?

But when A-dam heard the voice of God, he fear-ed and hid himself, and so did his wife, from the face of the Lord God. And they hid them-selves, al-so through shame, be-cause they were na-ked. And God said to A-dam, Who hath told thee that thou wast na-ked, but that thou didst eat of the tree of which I bade thee not to eat?

Then God said to him, For that thou hast heard the voice of thy wife, and didst eat of the fruit of the tree, curs-ed is the earth in thy work; with much toil shalt thou eat there-of all the days of thy life, till thou re-turn to the earth out of which I took thee; for dust thou art, and un-to dust thou shalt re-turn.

A-dam and Eve, by thus not o-bey-ing God, sinned, and by their sin they lost the grace and fa-vour of God. God then drove them out of the Gar-den of Pa-ra-dise, in which he had pla ced them; and he doom-ed them to die.

We are all born in-to this life with the guilt of their sin; that is call-ed o ri-gi-nal sin, be-cause as we des-cend and de-rive our life from them, so we also de-rive the guilt of their sin. We feel the sad effects of their sin, by the strong bent we find in us to sin, or to do wrong; and in the heat and cold, hun-ger and thirst, pains and toil, we suffer, and in death, through which we must all pass to the next life.

MORAL.

Oh! sad the fall of our first pa rents by sin! Thence learn, my child, how sad a thing it will be to you not to o-bey God, though in things that may seem light; take care that you do not sin by your own free will and choice, and dread the least sin. Flee those who would tempt or lead you to do evil.

LESSON IV.

Cain, Abel, Seth. The World drown-ed. No-e.

Gen. iv. 7.

A-dam and Eve had two sons; their names were Cain

and A bel. Cain till-ed the earth, A-bel took care of sheep in the fields. A-bel was good, and from his heart he served God : he of-fer-ed the best he had of his flock to God, and God was well pleas-ed with him. Cain was bad, and he did not of-fer the best of what he had to God, and God was not pleas ed with him.

Cain ha-ted A-bel be-cause God look-ed down kind-ly on him, and on what he of-fer-ed. One day when they both were in the fields, Cain rose up against Abel, and through en-vy kill-ed him. They who were born of Cain were bad like him-self.

Af-ter the death of A-bel, A-dam and Eve had a third son ; his name was Seth. He was good : like A-bel, he knew, lov-ed, and serv-ed God. His race, or they who were born of him, were al-so at first good ; but after a while they mix-ed with such as were bad of the race of Cain, and then they were bad like unto them.

Thence in a short time al-most the whole race of men and wo-men were bad. God was angry at them, and he meant to put an end to them, yet there was one good man whose name was No-e. God was well pleas-ed with him.

God then made it known to No-e, that he would drown the whole earth, and all that was on it ; but that he would save him and his wife and chil-dren, with a few of each kind of beasts and birds, in an ark which God bade him build. The ark was a kind of a trunk or ship made of wood. It was daub-ed in-side and out-side with pitch.

When the time was come that God would drown the earth, he made No-e go in-to the ark, and with him his wife, their three sons, and their wives ; and two or three of each sort of beasts and birds : as soon as they were in the ark, the door of it was shut.

It then rain-ed for for-ty days and for-ty nights, and all men, and wo-men, and chil-dren, and beasts and birds were drown-ed ex-cept No-e, and those with him in the ark. On-ly these eight per-sons of all man-kind were sav-ed. This is call-ed the De-luge.

By this you may judge, my child, how much God must hate sin, and them that com-mit it; at the same time how much he loves and how great care He takes of them that are good. Be then, my child good; love, fear, and serve God, and God will love and bless you, and take care that no harm come to you, while they that are bad feel the weight of his wrath.

Keep your-selves far off from bad boys and girls, and join such as are good; for with the good you will be good, but with the bad you will be bad, as it was with those of the race of good Seth; they were at first good as he was good; but as soon as they mix-ed with them that were bad, they were bad like un-to them.

LESSON V.

No-e goes out of the ark.   His three sons.

While No-e, and his wife, their three sons and their wives, were in the ark, the waters rose so high that all the hills were co-ver-ed, and all flesh died that mov-ed on the earth, both of fowl and of beasts, and of that which creep-ed upon the ground. And when they had been in the ark for the space of a year, the wa-ters be-gan to de-crease, till the earth was dry.

Then God spake to No-e, and said, Go forth out of the ark, thou and thy wife, and thy children. And No-e went forth out of the ark, and all that were with him. God bless-ed No-e and his sons, and pro-mis-ed that he would no more drown the earth; and he set the rain-bow as a sign there-of.

He gave in-to their hands, that is, he set them o-ver all the beasts of the earth, and the fowls of the air, and all the fish-es of the sea; and he said, They shall be meat for you; e-ven as the green herbs have I giv-en you all things; and while the earth re-mains, seed-time and har-vest, and cold and heat, and sum-mer and win-ter, and day and night shall not cease.

The three sons of No-e were Seth, Cham, and Ja-pheth. Seth and Ja-pheth were good, and had a great re-spect for their fa-ther; God there-fore bless-ed them. Cham was bad, and a bad deed drew up-on him-self the curse pro-phe-si-ed of God.

After the flood, when the land was dry, No-e till-ed it, and plant-ed the vine-tree. Of the fruit of that tree he made wine. When he had drunk of it, for he then did not know the strength of it, he fell a-sleep. Whilst he was a-sleep, he lay ex-pos-ed in a man-ner un fit to be seen.

When Cham saw his fa-ther na-ked, he look-ed on him and made a jest of him. He then told his bro-thers what he had seen. They blam-ed him for this deed, and dis-re-spect to their fa-ther. They then took a cloak, and, with their fa-ces turn-ed from their fa-ther, they cast it on him, and co-ver-ed him.

When No-e a-woke from sleep, and knew what had pass-ed, he blam-ed and chid-ed Cham, and laid a curse on Cha-na-an, the son of Cham. But he bless-ed Seth and Ja-pheth.

MORAL.

Learn here a-gain, my child, how sad a thing it is to sin and of-fend God. Dread the curse of God. Love and revere them of whom, next to God, you hold your life, and all that you have.

Do not, like many chil-dren, rail at them, nor make a jest of them in their old age. The curse of God falls on such chil-dren for their bad deeds. But he will bless those that love, o-bey, and re-spect their pa-rents.

LESSON VI.

The vain Scheme of the Chil-dren of No-e. Gen. xi.

No-e liv-ed af-ter the flood three hun-dred years; he saw the off-spring of his three sons who were with him in the ark grow to a great num-ber. The earth was then of one tongue, that is, they all spoke one and the same lan-guage. These, when they went from the east, found a plain, and dwelt in it.

They then said each to his neigh-bour, Come let us make brick, and bake them with fire; and let us build a town, and a tower, the top of which may reach as high as Hea-ven; and let us make our name great be-fore we dis-perse into all lands.

But God, who laughs at the at-tempts of men, when they think to op-pose His will, soon shew-ed them how vain, and void of force, they were in their scheme. He knew they would not cease to work while they all spoke one and the same tongue. He then so con-fus ed their speech, and they no long-er knew the one what an-o-ther said or call-ed for.

They were then for-ced to de-sist from their work. And that tow-er was call-ed, and is known by the name of Ba-bel, that is, of con-fu-sion ; be-cause there the tongue or speech of the whole earth was con-fus-ed, and of one it was chang-ed into many. Thence the Lord dis-pers-ed them up-on the face of all the coun-tries.

MORAL.

By this act and deed, you may see, my child, how vain it is for man to strive a-gainst God : He is great, and of such might, that no man can op-pose what He will, or will not, have done.

By the flood, and the change of speech, and by dis-pers-ing man-kind through-out the whole earth, He shew-ed that He is Lord of all, and that He can do what He pleas-eth, also, that He is wise and good, and does all for the good of man.

What love and praise then do we not owe Him ? Be-ware not to op-pose His will, but seek and pray to know it, and when you know it, beg Him to grant you His grace to com-ply with it.

And in all things that be-fall you, say, from your heart, O Lord, great and good, and wise and just ! Thy will be done. This done by the will and the hand of God, so be it, and may He be prais-ed.

LESSON VII.

A-bra-ham. Gen. xxv.

In a short time af-ter the de-luge, men lost all thought and fear of God. They e-ven did not own Him, who had by such great works made Him-self known to them to be God; but they set up for gods the very works of God. Such were the sun, fire, moon, and stars: to these they pray-ed; and they fell down before stocks and stones, which were the works of their own hands.

These they call-ed and held for gods. Their whole mind, and thought, and care, was for this life and the body ; like un-to brutes, they were led and rul-ed by their sen-ses. Hence they did not mind their souls, nor the things of God nor of the next life.

Such, my child, was the state of man-kind at that time : they liv-ed more like brutes, that know not God, than like men, whom God had made to know and to love him in this life, and af-ter this life to be hap-py with Him in Hea-ven. In this sad state would most men have been at this day, had not the good God by his grace pre-vent-ed it.

God then, to call men from their e-vil ways, and to keep them firm in the love and fear of Him, called forth a man who was good and just. His name was A-bra-ham. God pro-mis-ed him, if he would obey Him, that He would be a God to him, that is, he would bless him, and raise up a peo-ple from him, who should be His own peo-ple.

He would take care of them, and pre-serve in them, and by them, the know-ledge, love, and fear of Him, who was the on-ly one and true God. A-bra-ham be-liev-ed, and he did what-e-ver God bid him do. God also pro-mis-ed A-bra-ham, that of his seed or race, He should be born who should save the world.

MORAL.

Be-ware, my child, not so to mind the things of this world and life, as to bend to them your whole or chief care. If you do, you will lose the grace of God, and soon give in to the way of vice : and when you have lost the love and fear of God, then will your life be more the life of a brute than a man. See in A-bra-ham what love and care God hath of those who love and serve Him.

Hence, though you may chance to live with them that live as if they knew not God, nor love, nor fear Him, do you a-bide firm in your faith of Him, and in good life. De-part not by sin from God, and then He will be to you a God : he will bless you in this life, and

B3

in the next life He will make you happy with Him forever.

Lesson VIII.

The Faith and O-be-dience of A-bra-ham, I-sa-ac, E-sau, and Ja cob.

God made the choice of A-bra ham, before all men
of this time, that by him, He, the true God, might still be
known and served, though most men had lost all sense
of Him.   A-bra-ham had a son whom he much lov-ed.
His name was I-sa ac.   When I-sa-ac was grown up in
years, God, to try the faith of A-bra ham, or his be-lief
of what he had pro-mis-ed him, viz., that He who was
to save the world should be born of his seed, God called
to him, A-bra-ham! A-bra-ham! to whom A-bra-ham said,
Here I am.

God then bid him to put to death his son I-sa-ac,
whom he loved; for God, my child, is the Lord of man
and of his life.   A-bra-ham would have done it as soon
as God bade him; but just as he was up-on the point
of slay-ing his son I-sa-ac, an an-gel, or good spi-rit, sent on
the part of God, stopp-ed his hand, and thus the life of his
son was spar-ed.

I-sa-ac, like his father, was a good man.   He had
two sons: their names were E-sau and Jacob, and they
were twins, that is, both born at one and the same birth ;
E-sau was first born, but at the time Ja-cob came forth of
the womb, he held in his hand the plaint, or the sole of
E-sau's foot.

By this was meant, what af-ter-wards came to pass,
when E sau sold his birth-right for a mess of broth.   It
was thus Ja-cob sup-plant-ed, or, as it were, trip-ped
up the heel of his brother E-sau, and got from him his
birth-right.   Jacob was a good man, and when his fa-ther
was on his death-bed he bless-ed him.   But E-sau turn-ed
out bad.

Ja-cob had twelve sons.   They are known by the names
of the twelve Pa-tri-archs, or chief of twelve tribes.   And
God gave to Ja-cob the name of Is-ra-el, whence his race,
or they that sprang from him, were called Is-ra-el-ites.

MORAL.—Great and firm, you see my child, was the faith and trust of A-bra-ham in God; and prompt was his o-be-di-ence when he could have slain his son I-sa-ac; God wants not our goods, nor anything we can give, for all is His, and all comes from Him.

What He most seeks is our prompt will and heart to do His will, as soon as He makes it known to us: and He looks up on that as done which we would have done if such had been His will.

Hence A-bra-ham is styl-ed the Fa-ther of the Faith-ful, or of those who be-lieve in God. That you may be a true child of God, by faith be-lieve in Him, by hope trust in Him and through love o-bey Him, then will He bless you.

From E-sau learn, my child, how sad a thing it is to be too fond of, and to set our heart too much on, the things of this world. Such fond-ness blinds us, so that we no long-er know not what we love, nor what we lose.

That which we long for, and seek to have, is of-ten of no more va-lue than a mess of broth, if com-par-ed to the good things of the next life, that will have no end, which yet we lose with so much ease.

Observe.—When, my child, you read that God, or the Lord, call-ed to A-dam, or spoke to A-bra-ham, or do Mo-ses, or that they heard His voice, or saw Him, you are not to thnk that God did call or speak, or was heart, or seen in the same way as we speak, call, &c.

No, not so; but as God can do what He pleas-eth, and use such means as he may choose, to make known His will, or things, to us; He, by some voice or sound, brought to their ears and minds what He would have them, to know, hear, or do.

And if they say any thing which they thought to be God, it was not God whom they saw, for no man hath seen, or can see Him, but it was some-thing in the shape of man which they saw; and by these means God re-veal-ed to their minds, and re-pre-sent-ed to them, things as ful-ly and clear-ly, as if they re-al-ly saw Him, or heard His voice.

LESSON IX.

Jo-seph and his Bro-thers. Gen. xxxvii.

Of the twelve sons of Ja-cob, Jo-seph was dear-er to him than a ny of the rest. His bro-thers were griev-ed at it, and they hat-ed him. One day their fa-ther sent him to them, when they were in the fields with their flocks, to see if all things were well with them.

When he came to them, they said, Let us kill him. But one of them, by name Reu-ben, said, do not take his life from him, nor shed his blood, but cast him into this pit. They then strip-ped him of his coat, and cast him in-to the pit or well, which was dry.

And when some mer-chants pass-ed by that way, his bro-thers drew him out of the well, and they sold him to them. They brought him in-to E-gypt, and there they sold him to a prince, to be his slave.

Jo-seph was a man that in all things did so well, that his mas-ter made him dwell in the house, and he was in great fa-vour with him ; so far, that he was charg-ed with the care of all things, and he rul-ed in the house.

When he had been there a while, his master's wife wish-ed and press-ed him to do a great crime ; but Jo-seph was good, and fear-ed God, and he would by no means con-sent to do it. How can I com-mit a wick-ed thing, said he, and sin a-gainst my God! No. He then rush-ed from her.

She then charg-ed him false-ly with the crime, and he was cast into pri-son. When he had been there two years, the King sent for him to ex-plain him his dreams, Jo-seph ex-plain-ed them.

Then the King took his ring from his own hand, and gave it in-to the hand of Jo-seph ; he cloth-ed him with a silk robe, and put a chain of gold a-bout his neck; he made all bow their knee to him, and told them he was to rule the whole land of E-gypt.

Not long after, there was a dearth, or great want of corn, and Jo-seph had the care of all the corn. Ja-cob the fa-ther of Jo-seph, then sent his brothers to buy corn of him.

At first they did not know Jo-seph; and though he knew them, yet he feign-ed as if he did not know them, and he dealt with them as if they were spies. This he did to bring them by de-grees to a sense of their fault, when through en-vy they sold him; yet did Jo-seph love them.

He soon made him-self known to them. He wept through joy, kiss-ed them, and for-gave them. He then sent for his old fa-ther, who came to him. Jo-seph took care of him and his brothers. They lived in those parts; and when Ja-cob was dead, Jo-seph bu-ri-ed him in the place where he had de-si-red to be bu-ri-ed.

MORAL.

Thus you see, my child, that God doth not for-get nor for-sake them that fear and love Him. Though he some-times seems not to be mind-ful of them in their dis-tress, ye t in due time He comes to their aid and com-fort, and He makes all that be-falls them to turn to their good.

Be chaste, my child, like Jo-seph; do not stain your soul and life by an un-clean act, or thought, or look. Keep a guard up-on your eyes and heart, and flee those per-sons who would lead you to sin; ra-ther die than of-fend God. Like Jo-seph, for-get and for-give the wrongs done to you by an-o-ther. Re-vere your parents, take care of them, and help them all that you can in their old age, and in time of want, and at all times.

LESSON X.

Mo-ses. Ex-o-dus ii.

Mo-ses was an-o-ther great and good man. Soon af-ter he was born, his mother hid him for the space of three months. This she did to save him from be-ing put to death with o-ther chil-dren whom the King had or-der-ed to be kill-ed. When she could no long-er keep him hid, she made a bas-ket of bul-rush-es, and daub-ed it with pitch.— She then laid him in it, and set the bas-ket near the wa-ter's side.

When the king's daugh-ter came down to wash her-self, she es-pi-ed the bas-ket, and the child in it.—

She took him out of it and gave him to his own mother, though she was not known to be such, and she said
to her, Take this child and nurse him for me. When
he was grown up the King's daugh-ter a-dopt-ed him
for her son, and she gave him the name of Mo-ses, saying,
Be-cause from wa-ter did I take him. And she brought
him up.

MORAL.

- All this, my child, did not come to pass by chance;
no, such was the will of God, and His hand or power
brought all that about. Thus God, by ways and means
that seem strange to men, rules all things, and brings
them to pass as He pleas-eth, to the glo-ry of his name and
to our good. Thus you must think, and judge of all the
events in life.

LESSON XI.

The plagues of E-gypt. Ex. iii, vii, viii, ix.

God made use of Mo-ses to free his peo-ple from the
slave-ry un-der which Pha-ra-oh the King of E-gypt held
A-bra-ham, I-sa-ac, and Ja-cob, and were call-ed Is-ra-el-
ites. God shew-ed him-self to Mo-ses, or the glo-ry of
God ap-pear-ed to him in a flame of fire, out of the midst of
a bush. The bush burn-ed, yet did not waste.

And God, from the midst of the bush, call-ed to him,
Mo-ses! Mo-ses! Mo-ses, then said he, Here I am. And he
went to see the bush; but God said to him, Do not come
near; loose off thy shoes from thy feet, for the place on
which thou dost stand is ho-ly ground.

Then God said, I am the God of thy fa-ther, the God of
A-bra ham, the God of I-sa-ac, and the God of Ja-cob.
Mo ses then hid his face, for he durst not look at God.

Then God said to him, The cry of the chil-dren of
Is-ra-el, is come up to me. Come and I will send thee
un-to Pha.ra-oh, that thou may-est bring forth my peo-ple.
I will be with thee, and I will stretch out my hand, and I
will smite E-gypt with my won-ders.

These won-ders God did by Mo-ses to make the
king sub-mit to his will, and let his peo-ple go thence.—
They are call-ed the Plagues of E-gypt. Mo-ses struck,

with a rod that he held in his hand, the water in the river, and in-stant-ly it was chang-ed in-to blood.

He made frogs come and leap a-bout in all parts, e-ven in their houses. He brought a-mong them flies and gnats that bit them sore-ly. He brought a plague on the cat-tle, sores on men, a storm of hail, thick dark-ness that last-ed three days.

Last of all, God sent an an-gel who kill-ed all the first-born of the E-gyp-ti-ans, from the son of the king to the son of the mean-est slave. This last plague so fright-en-ed the King, that in the same hour he press-ed the Is-ra-el-ites to go forth and leave the coun-try; and they drove them out of the land of Egypt, and they load-ed them with rich-es.

MORAL.

Thus you see, my child, God can do, and doth, what He pleas-eth, and no one can with-stand Him. See a-gain, how dread-ful it is to har-den our hearts, and to shut our ears to the call and grace of God.

For, though God be good, yet He is just, and strong to strike, to punish us when we pro-voke Him by our ob-sti-nacy in sin-ning against Him. Love God, fear God, and do His will, that He may bless you.

LESSON XII.

The Is-ra-el-ites pass dry shod through the Red Sea.
Ex-o-dus, xiv.

No soon-er were the Is-ra-el-ites gone, than Pha-ra oh was vex ed that he had let them de-part. He then with his ar-my set out after them, to stop them. He came up to them on the banks of the Red Sea; and they then gave them-selves up for lost.

But Mo-ses stretch ed out his hand o-ver the sea, and in-stan-tly God made the sea o-pen, and the wa-ter re-tir-ed to each side, and stood like a wall on the right and the left, leav-ing a large and dry space in the midst through which the Is-ra-el-ites pass-ed dry-shod.

The E-gyp-ti-ans would fain have fol-low-ed them; but Mo-ses a-gain stretch-ed out his hand, and God made

the sea join its wa-ters, in which they were all drown.ed,
with Pha ra oh their king ; and they saw the E-gyp·ti·ans
dead on the shore.

Then Mo·ses and the Is-ra-el-ites sang to the Lord, and
said, Let us sing to the Lord.   My strength and my praise
is the Lord.   This is my God.   He hath drown·ed Pha-ra·oh
and his army in the Red Sea.   Who is like to Thee O God.

MORAL.

Thus, my child, God took care of his peo ple and sav·ed
them.   He shew-ed that he was Lord of all.   So will he
have care of you if you love and serve Him.

Put then, your whole trust in Him, call upon Him, pray
to Him, and he will save you from harm.   And when He
thus shews Him-self kind and care-ful of you, do you praise
and thank Him from your heart.   ᵥ

LESSON XIII.

The Jour-ney through the De-sert.   The Ten Command.
ments.   Ex. xvi, xix, xx.

When the Is-ra·el ites had pass ed the Red Sea, God led
them through a vast de-sert, or a wild and vast part of
land, in which no one dwelt.   This He did, to try if they
would be faith-ful to him, and to let them see that they
could not live with·out his care and kind ness.

A cloud led them the way by day, and it screen-ed them
from the heat of the sun.   At night it was chang-ed in-to
a pil-lar of fire, that serv-ed to light them.   For their food,
God gave them Man·na.   It was a kind of dew that fell
from the hea·vens ; and it was so thick that they made bread
of it.

When they were in want of drink, Mo·ses struck with
his rod a rock, out of which in-stantly there gush-ed forth
water.   Their clothes were not worn out, though their
jour·ney last·ed forty years.

Such care did God take of them ; yet they were un·grate-
ful to Him ; they long·ed to be a-gain in E·gypt, and they
were for kill-ing Mo-ses.

In the third month after they left E·gypt, they
came to Mount Si-na-i.   There God made them halt
a while, that He might give them His law.   When the
day was come on which they were to re ceive it,

they beheld the top of the moun-tain all on fire.

Then a thick cloud co-ver-ed it, and out of it broke forth dread-ful thun-der and light-ning. They heard a sound of trum-pets, and a great noise, but they saw no one. Then a loud and dread-ful voice broke forth out of the cloud, and spoke these words :

I am the Lord thy God, who brought thee out of the land of E-gypt, and out of the house of bond-age. Thou shalt not have strange Gods be-fore me. Thou shalt not make to thy-self a gra-ven thing, nor the like-ness of any-thing that is in hea-ven a-bove, or in the earth be-neath, or in the wa-ters un-der the earth. Thou shalt not a-dore nor serve them.

I am the Lord thy God, strong and jea-lous, vi-sit-ing the sins of the fa-thers up-on their chil-dren, to the third and fourth ge-ne-ra-tion, of them that hate me ; and shew-ing mer-cy to thou-sands of those that love me, and keep my com-mand-ments.

Thou shalt not take the name of the Lord thy God in vain ; for the Lord will not hold him guilt-less that shall take the name of the Lord his God in vain.

Re-mem-ber that thou keep ho-ly the Sab-bath day.— Six days shalt thou work, and shalt do all thy works.— But on the sev-enth day is the Sab-bath of the Lord thy God : thou shalt do no work on it, thou, nor thy son, nor thy daughter, nor thy man-ser-vant, nor thy wo-man-ser-vant, nor thy beast, nor the stranger that is with in thy gates.

Forin six days the Lord made hea-ven and earth, and the sea, and all things that are in them, and rest-ed on the sev-enth : there-fore the Lord bless ed the Sab-bath day and sanc-ti-fi-ed it.

Ho-nour thy fa-ther and thy mo-ther that thou may-est live long up-on the earth which the Lord thy God will give thee. Thou shalt not mur-der. Thou shalt not com-mit a-dul-te-ry. Thou shalt not steal.

Thou shalt not speak a-gainst thy neigh-bour false tes-ti-mony. Thou shalt not co-vet thy neigh-bours house, nei-ther shalt thou desire his wife, nor ser-vant, nor han-maid, nor ox, nor ass, nor a-ny-thing that is his.

These are the Ten Com-mand-ments which God pub-lish-
ed to his peo-ple; and he gave them writ-ten on two tables of stone to Mo-ses, who was at that time on the Mount
in the clouds.

Though by the thun-der and light-ning God would move
them and us to care-ful keep-ing of them, yet His will is
rather that we grave them in our hearts, and keep them
not so much through our fear, as through our love of Him.

Keep them, my child, all the days of your life, and you
will please God, and He will bless you here, and after this
life you will see him in all his glo-ry, and en-joy Him for
e-ver.

LESSON XIV.

Da-vid and Go-li-ah, 1 Kings, xvii.

The peo-ple of God had for a long time been rul-ed by
Judg-es. At length, they de-sir-ed to have Kings. Their
first king was Saul. In his reign he fought ma ny bat-
tles. And in his time there came forth from the camp of
the Phil-is tines, who were e ne-mies to the Is ra el-ites, a
man whose name was Go li-ah.

He was six cu bits, that is, three yards, or nine feet,
and a span high. He had on his head a hel-met of brass,
and he was arm ed with a coat of mail of ve-ry great
weight; he had greaves of brass on his leg; and a staff in
his hand which was like a large beam.

This huge man stood day after day and cried to the Is-
ra-el-ites. Choose out a man of you, and let him come
down to me. If he be a-ble to fight with me, and to kill
me, then will we be your servants; but if I kill him, then
shall ye be our ser-vants, and serve us.

Now there was a man whose name was Jesse, and he
had eight sons. The youugest of them was call-ed Da-
vid. He used to tend his fa-ther's sheep. One morn ing
he rose up ear-ly and went to the camp. At the same time
came Go-li ah.

When the men of Is-ra-el saw the man, they were
a fraid, and fled from him. And they said to Da-vid,

Have you seen this man that is come to defy us? David said to the men who stood by him, What shall be done to the man that shall kill Go-li-ah?

And they said to him, To the man who kill-eth Go-li-ah the king will give great rich-es and his daugh-ter, and he will make his father's house free.

Da-vid then went to Saul, and said to him, Let no man's heart fail be-cause of Go-li-ah: thy servant will go and fight with him. Saul said to Da-vid, Thou art not a-ble to fight with him, for thou art but a strip-ling, but he is a man trained to war from his youth.

Da-vid said to Saul, I kept my fa-ther's sheep, and there came a li-on and a bear, that took a lamb out of the flock; and I went out and I smote them. I slew both the li-on and the bear; and this man shall be as one of them.

Da-vid al-so said, The Lord, who sav-ed me out of the paw of the li-on, and out of the paw of the bear, He will save me out of the hand of this man. And Saul said to Da-vid Go, and the Lord be with thee.

Then Saul cloth-ed Da-vid with a coat of mail, und put a hel-mit of brass up-on his head. When Da-vid was thus cloth-ed, and gird-ed with a sword, he tried if he could go thus armed; but he said to Saul, I cannot go so; and he put them off.

He then took his staff, and he choose five smooth bright stones out of the brook, and he cast them in-to his scrip. Then he took a sling in his hand, and went forth a-gainst Go-li-ah.

When Go-li-ah saw Da-vid, he said to him, Am I a dog, that thou com-est to me with a staff? come to me, and I will give thy flesh to the fowls of the air, and to the beasts of the earth.

Then Da-vid said to him. Thou com-est to me with a spear, and a sword, and a shield; but I come to thee in the name of the Lord of Hosts. The Lord of the bands of Is-ra-el, whom thou hast this day de-fied, He, the Lord, shall give thee in-to my hands, and I shall strike thee, and take a-way thy head from thee.

And I shall give the car-cas-ses of the camp of the Phil-is-tines to the fowls of the air and to the beasts of the earth, that all the earth may know there is a God in Is-ra-el. And all here shall know that not in the sword, nor in the spear, doth the Lord save ; for it is His bat-tle, and He will give thee in-to our hands.

Then Go-li-ah rose up, and came a-gainst Da-vid. Da-vid then put his hand in-to his scrip, and took one stone, and cast it with a sling, and struck Go-li-ah on the fore-head, who fell on his face up-on the ground. And where-as Da-vid had no sword, he ran and stood upon Go-li-ah, and he took his sword, and with it he slew him and cut off his head.

Da-vid then took Go-li-ah's head and he brought it in-to Je-ru sa-lem. Then Ab-ner, the prince of the army, took Da-vid, and he brought him to Saul, having in his hand the head of Go-li-ah. Saul took Da-vid that day, and would let him go no more home to his father's house. And David went out whi-ther-so-e-ver Saul sent him : and he be-hav-ed wise-ly ; and Saul placed him over the men of war, and he was ac-cept-ed in the eyes of the peo-ple.

MORAL.

Thus a-gain you see, my child, that God doth what He pleas-eth. The weak he makes strong, and the strong he ren-ders weak. Da-vid fights, and acts in the name, and by the strength of God, and not in his own.

If we trust in God, and not in our own strength, He will be for us, and help us ; and if He be for us, and with us, who or what can hurt us ? what have we to fear !

But as with-out Him we are no-thing, so with-out Him we can do no-thing. He hates the proud and ar-ro-gant ; but He looks down on the humble, and to them He gives His grace, by which they might do great things.

Lesson XV.

David made King. 2 Kings, ii.

After the death of Saul, Da-vid was cho-sen King. He was a great man, as you have seen ; and was also a good man. He in-deed sin-ned against God by two great crimes, mur-der and a-dul-te-ry; but he re-pent-ed of them, su-ed to God to par-don him, and God did par-don him. He then lov-ed, fear-ed, and serv-ed God all the days of his life, with his whole heart. Da-vid was al-so a man of bright parts, and well skill-ed in mu-sic and po-e-sy. He com-pos-ed a great num-ber of can-ti-cles, or songs, in praise of God. These are the Psalms which are sung to this day in the Church.

God made known to him, that He who was to save the world should be born of his race, and that He should be a king, and reign, not on ly over the house of Is-ra-el, but o-ver all the na-tions of the Earth and that of his king-dom there should be no end; that He (the Sa-vi-our of the World) should be the Son of God, and God him-self. All this was re-veal-ed by God to Da-vid.

The Is-ra-el-ites nam-ed the Re-deem-er, whom they ex-pect-ed, as the Jews do to this day, the Mes-si-ah, or the Christ. By the name is meant a-noint-ed, be-cause it was u-su-al to a-noint with oil those who were made Kings, Priests and Pro-phets; and Christ was a King, a Priest and a Pro phet. They like-wise call ed him the Son of Da-vid.

MORAL.—Thus, my child, those who seem, in the eyes of men, to be mean, poor, and low, and of no ac-count, are made use of by God to bring a-bout the great ends of His love, good-ness, and mer-cy, to sin-ful men.

The fool-ish things of the world hath God cho-sen to con-found the wise; and the weak things of the world that he may con-found the strong; and the base things of the world hath God cho-sen, and things that are not, that he might bring to naught things that are, that no flesh should glo-ry in His sight.

If a-ny time, my child, you of-fend God by sin, de-lay not to re turn to Him: be sor-ry, crave his mercy, and beg his par-don, and re-solve not to sin a-gain.

LESSON XVI.

The In-car-na-tion and Birth of Je-sus.

You have read, my child, that our first pa-rents

A-dam and Eve, lost, by their sin, the grace and fa-vour of God, and were dri-ven out of Pa-ra-dise. They more-o-ver were not, after this life, to have been hap-py with God in hea-ven : and, as we all sin-ned in them, we were to have been in the like sad state, had not God shew-ed mer-cy to them and to us.

He there-fore took pi-ty on man-kind, and sent His Son to re-deem us from sin, and to save us from hell. This Son was he whom God had pro-mis-ed to A-dam, A-bra-ham, Ja-cob and Da-vid : but he did not come till four thou-sand years af-ter the fall of A-dam and Eve.

Now his birth was after this man-ner : When the time ap-point-ed by God was come, God sent from hea-ven an an-gel, whose name was Ga-bri-el, to a young vir-gin, whose name was Ma-ry. She was of the race of Da-vid. The an-gel in-form-ed her from God that she should bring forth, and be the mo-ther of, the Mes-si-ah, Christ, or Re-deem-er.

Thou shalt have a Son, said the an-gel to Ma-ry, and thou shalt call his name Jesus. He shall be great, and shall be call-ed the Son of the Most High. She gave her con-sent, and in-stant-ly she con-ceiv-ed in her womb Christ. He that was God, took flesh, and our na-ture, and be-came like to us, though not with sin and ig-no-rance. And he was born of her in Beth-le-hem, a small town, where Da-vid had his birth.

His mo-ther, the bless-ed Vir-gin Ma-ry, and his fos ter or re-put-ed fa-ther, Saint Jo-seph, at that time were on their jour-ney, and as there was no room for them in the inns, they were con-strain-ed to lodge in a sta-ble. In that poor place, she brought forth in-to the world, her son Christ, who was to save the world. She wrap-ped Him in swad-dling clothes, and laid him in a man-ger.

And there were in the same coun-try, shepherds, watch-ing, and keep-ing the night watch-es o-ver their flocks. And, be-hold, an an-gel of the Lord stood by them and the bright-ness of God shone round a-bout them, and they fear-ed with a great fear.

And an an-gel said to them, Fear not, for be-hold I bring you good tid-ings of great joy that shall be to all the peo-ple; for this day is born to you a Sa-vi-our, who is Christ, the Lord, in the ci ty of Da vid; and this shall be a sign to you, you shall find the in-fant wrap ped in swad-dling clothes, and laid in a man-ger.

And sud-den-ly there was with the an-gel a mul ti-tude of the hea-ven-ly host prais-ing God, and say-ing, Glo-ry be to God in the high-est, and on earth peace to men and good will. And it came to pass, af-ter the an-gel de-part-ed from them in-to bea-ven, the shep-herds said one to an-o-ther, Let us go o-ver to Beth-le-hem, and let us see this Word that is come to pass, which the Lord hath shew-ed us.

And they came with haste, and they found Ma-ry and Jo-seph and the in-fant ly-ing in the man-ger; and see-ing, they un-der-stood of the Word that had been spo ken to them con-cern-ing this child. And the shep-herds re-turn-ed glori-fy-ing and prais-ing God for all the things they had heard and seen, as it was told unto them.

MORAL.

This, my child is the great work of God, out of His pure love to us. The word was made flesh, the Son of God be-came man, and he dwelt a-mong us. A-dore and praise him, and give him thanks. In his birth he is poor and as the out cast of men. If then you be poor, re-pine not at your state, since Christ was poor for your sake.

LESSON XVII.
Of Christ af-ter his Birth.

ON the eighth day af-ter Christ was born, he was called JE-SUS, or Sa-vi our. At this name we bow our heads, to give him a mark of our res-pect, as our Lord; and of our love and thanks as our Re deem er.

At the name of JE-SUS let every knee bow. Short-ly af-ter, three kings, or wise men came out of the east to a-dore Him.

They were guid-ed on their way by a bright star un-til it came and stood o-ver where the child Je-sus was. And en-ter-ing in-to the house, they found the child with Ma-ry his mo-ther; and fall-ing down, they a-dor-ed him; and o-pen-ing their trea-sures, they offer-ed him gifts —gold, frank-in-cense, and myrrh.

Up-on this, King He-rod, through jea lousy, would have put him to death: and to that end he gave or-ders that all the male chil dren, in and a-bout Beth le-hem, of the age of two years, should be slain; and they were killed. These are call-ed the Ho-ly In-no-cents.

But Christ was saved; for an an-gel of the Lord ap-pear-ed to Jo-seph, while a-sleep, and said, A-rise, and take the child and his mo-ther, and flee in-to E gypt, and there be un-til I shall tell thee: for it will come to pass that He-rod will seek the child to des-troy him. And they did not re-turn to the land of Is-ra-el till after the death of He rod.

At the age of twelve years, Je-sus went with his pa-rents to Je ru-sa lem, for the feast of the Pas-so-ver; there they lost him; and on the third day they found him in the Tem-ple seat-ed a-midst the doc-tors hear-ing them, and ask-ing them ques-tions. He then re-turn-ed with them to Na-za-reth, and liv-ed sub-ject to them; and he ad-van-ced in wis-dom, and in age, and in grace be-fore God and man.

MORAL.

Af-ter the ex-am-ple of Je sus, you must en-dea-vour, as you ad-vance in age, al so to ad vance in vir-tue and pi-e ty. To that end, be di-li gent at school; there hear your teach ers, be sub-ject to them, and to your pa-rents, and let no day pass with-out pray-ing to God; beg of Him to give you His grace to know Him more and more; to love Him more and more, and to serve Him more and more faith-ful-ly.

LESSON XVIII.
The Mi-ra-cles of Je-sus Christ.

Af-ter Je-sus re-turn-ed to Na-za-reth with his pa-rents, we read lit-tle more of him; but he liv-ed un-known to the age of thir-ty years. At that age he was bap-tiz-ed by Saint John, who is there-fore call-ed the Bap-tist. He then went in-to a de-sert, and there he fast-ed for-ty days,

Af-ter that, he came forth, and he chose twelve poor men ; these are call.ed the A pos-tles ; that is to say, en-voys, or per-sons sent, be-cause he sent them to preach and teach the Gos pel. Je sus, in the course of three years, wrought a great ma-ny mi-ra-cles ; that is, he did those things which no man can do.

But as he was God as well as man, he could do all what-e-ver he pleased, he cur-ed all sorts of dis-eas es, the fe-ver, the flux of blood, the drop-sy, the pal-sy, the le-pro-sy, of-ten by a word, and when he was not near' the sick per-son.

He gave sight to the blind ; he made the dumb speak, the deaf hear, the lame walk ; he brought to life those who were dead ; a-mong these we read in par-ti-cu-lar of a young girl who was just dead ; a young man whom his mo-ther was con-vey-ing to the grave ; and La-za-rus, who had been bu-ri-ed four days.

He was seen to walk on the sea ; and he made Saint Pe-ter do the like. One day he fed five thousand per-sons with five loaves of bread and two fish-es ; an-o-ther time he fed four thou-sand with sev-en loaves. He knew the thoughts of men.

All these won-ders prov-ed that he was, as he said of him-self, the Christ, and the Son of God. And three of his dis-ci-ples heard a voice from hea-ven that said of him, This is my be-lo-ved Son, in whom I am well pleas ed ; hear ye him.

MORAL

You must, my child, hear him when he speaks to you, and makes his will known to you by the voice of your pa-rents and teach-ers, for if you hear and o-bey them, you hear and o-bey him.

It is by them God will shew you what you must do to please Him, and to save your soul. If you do these things, he will be pleas-ed with you, and bless you, and af-ter your death, He will make you happy with Him in hea-ven.

LESSON XIX.

The Vir-tues of Je-sus Christ.

At the same time Je-sus did all those mi-ra-cles,

c

He gave an ex-am-ple of all sorts of virtues. He was hum-ble, meek, kind and good to all. He went a-bout do-ing good to all. He was not vain nor proud. He said, I seek not my own glo ry. I do the things that are pleas-ing to my Fa-ther. I do the will of Him who sent me.

Though he was the Son of God, yet He call-ed him-self the Son of Man. He de-part-ed from those who would fain have made him their King. One day some chil-dren were pre-sent-ed to him ; he em-brac-ed them, and bless ed them. He pass-ed his life in po-ver-ty and want, not hav-ing land nor house, nor so much as a place where to rest his head.

He suf-fer-ed, heat cold, hun-ger, thirst, and fa-tigue. He of-ten pass-ed the whole night in pray-er. My meat, he said, is to do the will of Him who sent me. When re-vil-ed, call-ed an im-pos-ter, se-du-cer, glut-ton, he did not re-vile again, but bore all in sil-ence.

MORAL.

En-dea-vour, my child, to co-py in you the life and vir-tues of Je-sus; shun pride and vain glo-ry. In all your thoughts, words, and ac-tions, seek only the glo-ry of God, not the es teem of them.

Be meek, and rea-dy to serve and do good to e-ve-ry one, e-ven to the poor-est wretch on earth. Love God, and serve God, be-cause such is the will of God, and he hath made you for that end.

Lesson XX.
The doc-trine of Je-sus Christ.

Learn now, my child, the truths which Je-sus taught, and which you must be-lieve if you would please God, and save your soul. God has made you and plac-ed you in this world, to know, love, and serve Him. It is then by faith you must know Him, and be-lieve all that He teach-es ; by hope you must re-ly on Him, for his grace and help, to live well, and by cha-ri-ty, you are to love him a-bove all things.

These are the three chief vir-tues. Je-sus teach-eth that life e-ver-last-ing, or the way to gain it, is to know God, the on-ly true God, and him-self Jesus

Christ, whom God hath sent to re-deem us, and teach us.

He teach-eth that He and the Fa-ther are but one; hence that he is God, as his Fa-ther is God; and he tells his A-pos-tles that he will send them the Spi-rit, who pro-ceeds from the Fa-ther; and he adds he shall re-ceive of mine, to teach it you; be-cause all that is the Fa-ther's is mine. This shews, that the Holy-Ghost or Spi-rit pro-ceeds from the Fa-ther and from the Son, and yet that all three, the Fa-ther, the Son, and the Holy Ghost, are but one and the same God.

And as Je-sus is God, it fol-lows that He is both God and Man, since he took to him-self the na-ture of man. And He shows it clear-ly, when He saith, No one hath as-cend-ed in-to hea-ven, but He who is come down from hea-ven, the Son of Man who is in hea-ven.

These truths, my child, are the ground-work of your faith, or be-lief. They are called the My ste-ries of the U-ni-ty, or of One God, and of the Tri-ni-ty, or of Three per-sons in One God, and of God the Son tak-ing flesh, and be-ing made man.

They are call-ed My-ste-ries, that is, se-cret truths, hid-den from us, or what are a-bove our know-ledge, or com-pre-hen-sion; yet must we be-lieve them, be-cause God, who is truth it-self, hath re-veal-ed them, and Je-sus Christ hath taught them. And as God is all-wise and good, He there-fore can-not be de-ceiv-ed, nor de-ceive us.

That your faith of these truths may in-crease and be firm, of-ten make this, or the like act of faith. O God, I be-lieve Thou art the only true God! O Je-sus Christ; I be-lieve Thou art the Son of the liv-ing God, who cam-est down from hea ven and wast made Man for us and our sal-va-tion. O Ho-ly Ghost, I be-lieve Thou art the Di vine Spi-rit pro-ceed-ing from the Fa-ther and the Son; and with them, One and the same God. O bless-ed Tri-ni-ty, One God.

LESSON XXI.

The max-ims of Je-sus Christ.

JE-SUS CHRIST teach-eth us, that of our-selves, and

with-out Him, we can do no-thing. As it `is in God, and by God, that we live, move, and are, so it is on-ly by His grace and help that we can do good un-to our e-ter-nal sal-va-tion. As the branch can-not bear fruit if it do not a-bide on the tree, so nei-ther can we bring forth the fruit of good works, if we do not a-bide in God by faith, hope, and love, and He give us not His grace.

Christ saith, speak-ing of him-self, I am the way, the truth, and the light. He is the way, in what he teach es by His word and by His life which we must co-py. He is the truth, by what he pro-mis-es; and He is the life by the grace which we re-ceive through Him, and we have need of this grace; for he saith, No man can come to me, un-less the Fa-ther who hath sent me, draw him.

This grace is His free gift; hence we must beg it of God. Ask, saith he, and it shall be giv-en to you: seek, and you shall find. And it is He who must teach us how to pray, and what to ask. Thus he teach-eth us. When you pray, say, Our Fa-ther, who art in Hea-ven, &c. This pray-er is call-ed the Lord's Pray-er.

He more-o-ver teach-es us not to con fine our hope to the earth, and to this life; for we are here but for a short time; for a few years or days, as it may please God, who is the Lord of the life of man. We are not then to heap up rich-es here, but to lay up a trea-sure in hea-ven by a life of good works.

He tells us, there are two ways, and two gates: but that we must strive to en-ter at the nar-row gate, and walk in the straight way; for this leads to life, but is found by few, be-cause there are few who choose it; the great-er part of men pre-fer the broad way that leads to death and ru-in.

To fol-low Je-sus in the straight and nar-row way to hea-ven, we must, my child, re-nounce the de-vil, and his works of sin; the world and its pomps; the flesh and its baits. We must car-ry the cross by the prac-tice of virtue. We must love God, and keep his com-mand-ments. If we do this, we shall af ter our death en-ter in-to life e-ver-last-ing, and be hap-py for e-ver with God.

For my child, there will come a day and an hour when you must die, and leave this world and all that is in it; for since A-dam sin-ned we are all doom-ed to die; and when we are dead, our bo-dies will be laid un-der ground, and they will mould-er in-to dirt and dust.

But our souls will be judg-ed by God, and ac-cord ing as we have liv-ed well or ill in this life, we shall live for e-ver ei-ther in hap-pi-ness or mi-se ry, be-yond what can be en-joy ed or en-dur-ed in this life, or what we are a-ble to con-ceive. The souls of some who have not been ve-ry good dur-ing part of their life time, and yet have had par-don of their sins, will go in-to a pri-son call-ed Pur ga-to-ry, for a while.

And at the last day, all that are in the graves will hear the voice of the Son of God, and they will come from their graves to be judg ed by him pub-li-cly, of all their thoughts, words and deeds, done in this life, good and bad. And they who have done good, will then go bo-dy and soul to a life of hap-pi-ness that will ne-ver end, of such joy and of such good things as no man ev-er saw, or can con-ceive; and they who have done e-vil will be cast bo-dy and soul in-to hell fire.

To one of these ends, you my child must one day come. Live well, then, that you may die well; for as you live, so you will die, and be hap-py or mi-ser-a-ble for ev-er after death. This is the sum of what Je-sus taught, and of what you must be-lieve and prac-tice till death. Be wise then, now in time; for when the hour of your death is come it will be too late to set a-bout it; you may then wish to do, and to have done well; but wish-es then will be in vain.

Lesson XXII.

The Suf-fer-ings and Death of Je-sus Christ

THOUGH Je-sus was much fol-low-ed and ad-mir-ed, for peo-ple came from all parts to see and hear Him, yet there were some who hat-ed Him so far as to seek His death. And, though in the whole course of His life He did no harm, but was good and kind to all, yet He was ill-treat-ed.

More than once the Jews took up stones to stone Him, They re-proach-ed Him, say-ing, He hath a de-vil, and was mad. If then Je-sus was so ill-treated, learn from Him to bear pa-ti-ent-ly what ill-treat-ment may be-fall you, and for-give them that hate you, or do you any wrong.

At length the Jews were re-sol-ved to take a-way his life. It was at the time of the Pass-over, a great feast ob-serv-ed by them, they con-triv-ed to do it. But be-fore they did it, Je-sus, when he was at his last sup-per, with his dis-ci-ples, the night be-fore He di-ed, gave them his bo-dy and blood in this man-ner :

He took bread in-to his hands ; He bless-ed it, and broke it. He then gave his bo-dy to them, and said, Take and eat ; This is my bo-dy. He then gave them his blood thus: He took the cup with some wine and wa-ter in it, and said to them, Take and drink ; This is my blood. When He did this, He in-sti-tut-ed the Sa-cra-ment of the Ho-ly Eu-cha-rist, and the Sa-cri-fice of the Mass.

After He had done this, He went forth in-to a gar-den, and there He pray-ed to his Fa-ther. Father! if it be pos-si-ble, let pass from me this cha-lice (by which He meant his pas-sion and death,) yet, not as I will, but as Thou wilt ; Thy will be done.

Whilst He was thus pray-ing, Ju-das, one of his dis-ci-ples, brought with him arm-ed men to seize Je-sus.—They seiz-ed Him, and thus led Him to Cai-phas, the High Priest. From Cai-phas they led Him to Pi-late ; from Pi-late to He-rod and again to Pi-late.

They blind-fold-ed Him, scoffed at Him, spit in his face, strip ped off his clothes, and ti-ed Him to a pil-lar ; there they scourg-ed Him ; they then cloth-ed Him with an old pur-ple gar-ment, put a reed in-to his hand, and a crown of thorns on his head ; set. Him on a stool, and then a-dor-ed Him as a mock king. Af-ter all this cru-el treat-ment, they nailed Him by his hands and his feet to a cross. This was done at noon day.

He hung on the cross in great pain and a-go-ny un-til three o'clock in the af-ter-noon, when He ex-pir-ed. Thus di-ed Je-sus to save the world. At His death the sun was dark-en-ed, rocks were split, and the dead rose from their graves.

Oh! my child, how great must have been the ev-il of the sin of our first pa-rents! since to re-deem us from it, to re-con-cile man-kind to God, and to set hea-ven o-pen to us, Christ, the Son of God, made man, suf fer-ed so much and at last died on the cross!

Great was his love for us. Love him then, and through love of Him see you do not com-mit sin. Hate and de-test it as the worst thing that can be-fall you in this life. Of-ten think on what Je-sus hath done and suf-fer-ed for you; praise and thank Him; and beg you may reap the fruit of it by his grace here, and by e-ter-nal hap-pi-ness here-af-ter.

LESSON XXIII.

The Bu-ri-al, Re-sur-rec-tion, and As-cen sion of Je-sus Christ, and the Ge-ne-ral Judg-ment of Man-kind.

WHEN Je-sus was dead, they laid his bo-dy in a se-pul-chre, or grave; and on the third day af-ter his death, He rais-ed Him-self from death to Life. He ap-pear-ed of-ten to his dis-ci-ples for the space of for-ty days. The last time He ap-pear-ed to them was on Mount O-li-vet: there af-ter He had spo-ken to them, He lift-ed up His hands, and bless-ed them.

Then He as-cend-ed up to hea-ven in their pre-sence, till a cloud took Him out out of their sight. Then two an-gels in the form of men, cloth-ed in white robes, told them, that He should one day come a-gain in like man-ner as they had seen Him go up to hea-ven.

Then it was that Je-sus Christ took pos-ses-sion of His king-dom, of which there will be no end. And there He sit-teth at the right hand of God the Fa-ther; not that God hath hands, for He is a pure spi-rit with-out mat-ter, form, or fi-gure; by this is meant, Christ is rais-ed, as Man, a-bove all that is in hea-ven; and to the high-est glo-ry and dig-ni-ty; for, as God, He is one and the same God with the Fa-ther.

There He will con-ti-nue in that state till He come at the last day, when an end will be put to this world, to judge the liv-ing and the dead; those who are now dead, we who are now liv-ing, but shall die; and those who will be li-ving at the last day, but al-so will first die; for it is ap-point-ed un-to all men once to die, and then the judg-ment.

For the hour will come, when all that are in the graves shall hear the voice of the Son of God, and they shall come forth; they that have done good un-to the re sur-rec-tion of the life, and they that have done e-vil un-to the re-sur-rec-tion of the judg-ment.

For God hath ap-point-ed a day, in which He will judge the world in jus-tice by that man, the Son of God, Je-sus Christ, whom He hath or-dain-ed, where-of He hath given as-su-rance to all men, in that He rais-ed Him from the dead; and af-ter that the judg-ment. all things will be per-fect-ly sub-ject-ed to Him, and the de-signs of God from all e-ter-ni ty will be en-tire-ly ac-com plish-ed.

LESSON XXIV.
The Es-tab-lish-ment of the Church.

BUT af-ter Je-sus was as cend-ed in-to Hea-ven, He thence sent down, ac-cord-ing to his pro-mise be-fore He was put to death, the Pa-ra-clete or Com-fort-er, the Di-vine Spi-rit or the Ho-ly Ghost, to en-light-en the minds of His A-pos-tles and Dis-ci-ples, that they might un-der-stand all that which He, when li-ving with them on earth, had taught them, and would then bring to their minds.

Al-so to con-firm them in the faith or be-lief of such truths, and to en-able them to teach them, and to preach the Gos-pel through out the whole world; and more-o-ver, to con-firm the same by the mi-ra-cles which they should work in his name, and by his pow-er.

This came to pass thus: When the days of Pen-te-cost were ac-com-plish-ed, the A-pos-tles and Dis-ci-ples of Christ were all to-gether in one place; and sud-den-ly there came a sound from Hea-ven as of a migh-ty wind com-ing, and it fill-ed the whole house where they were sit-ting ; and there ap-pear-ed to them part-ed tongues, as it were of fire, and it sat o-ver e ve ry one of them ; and they were all fill-ed with the Ho-ly Ghost.   Acts ii.

It was thus Je-sus Christ es-tab-lish-ed his Church.— And *all they that be-liev-ed were to-ge-ther—they con tin-u-ed dai-ly with one ac-cord in the Tem-ple—And the Lord add-ed dai-ly to them such as should be sav ed.*   Acts ii.— And then was ful-fill-ed what Je-sus had said, that they who be-liev-ed on Him should do still great-er works than He him-self had done.

With this his Church He pro-mis-ed the same Di-vine Spi-rit should al-ways a bide ; and teach and guide her (the Church) in all truths un-to the end of the world: in such sort that the gates of Hell, or Satan, should ne-ver pre-vail a-gainst her, in-duce her to be-lieve, or to teach the least er-ror.

The truth and fact of this were de mon s r t ed be yond all doubt, by the ma-ny mi-ra-cles, and signs and won-ders which the fol-low-ers of Je-sus did e-ve-ry where through his pow-er, and in his name ; be-cause to him was giv-en all pow-er in hea-ven and on earth, un-to the e-ter-nal sal-va-tion of all them that should be-lieve in Him, and-be-lieve in the Ho-ly Ca-tho-lic Church, which He had es tab-lish-ed:

In this man-ner, and by the tes-ti-mo-ny which the A-pos-tles and Dis-ci-ples of Je-sus Christ, and the in-nu-me-ra-ble Mar-tyrs, gave of the truths of the Gos-pel and of the Church of Je-sus Christ, by the blood which they shed, and by their lives which they vo-lun-ta-ri ly laid down un-der the most cru-el tor-ments, God set, as it were, his seal to the tes-ti mo-ny, that all which Je-sus had taught was true and di-vine.

And this held, and still holds and will hold un-to the end of the world, the fol-low-ers of Je-sus Christ.   Chris-tians and Ca-tho-lics, the mem-bers of his Church, firm and stea-dy in the faith and com-mu-ni-on of One, Ho-ly, Ca-tho-lic, and A-pos-to-lic Church ; in which Church a-lone are to be ob tain-ed for-give ness of sins here, and here-af-ter a glo-ri-ous re sur-rec-tion, and e-ver-last-ing,

by means of the Ho-ly Sa-cri-fice, Sa-cra-ment, &c., &c.
in-sti-tu-ted and or-daio-ed by Christ him-self.

TABLE IX.

Words of Three Syllables, accented on the First.

Ab sti nence	at tri bute	ca" te chism
ab di cate	au di ence	ca" tho lic
ab ro gate	a" ve nue	ce" le brate
ab so lute	Ba" che lor	cen tu ry
ac ci dent	bail a ble	cham pi on
ac cu rate	bar bar ous	chan cel lor
ac tu ate	bar ris ter	cha rac ter
ad e quate	bar ren ness	chy" mi cal
ad jec tive	bash ful ness	chy" mis try
ad" ju tant	bat te ry	cho ris ter
ad ju gate	bat tle ment	cin na mon
ad mi ral	beau ti ful	cir cum flex
ad vo cate	blun der buss	cir cum spect
af fa ble	blun der ing	cla mour ous
af flu ence	blus ter er	clas si cal
ag gra vate	bois ter ous	clean li ness
al der man	book bind er	cle" men cy
al pha bet	bor row er	cog ni zance
al ti tude	bot tom less	co gen cy
am nes ty	boun ti ful	co" lo ny
am pli fy	bre" vi ty	co lo quy
an cho ret	bro ther ly	com bat ant
an nu al	bur gla ry	com pa ny
a" nar chy	but ter fly	com pe tent
an ces tor	Cal cu late	com pli ment
a" ni mate	ca" lum ny	com pro mise
a" pa thy	ca" len dar	con fer ence
ap pe tite	can di date	con fi dence
a po logue	cap ti vate	con flu ence
a" que duct	car di nal	com fort less
ar bi trate	car ti lege	con gru ous
ar chi tect	care ful ly	con quer or
ar gu ment	car mel ite	con se crate
ar ma ment	car pen ter	cor pu lent
ar ro gant	ca ta logue	cost li ness
as pi rate	ca" ta ract	coun sel lor

con so nant
con sta ble
con stan cy
con sti tute
con tra band
con tra ry
con ver sant
cor mo rant
cor po ral
coun ter pane
coun ter feit
coun ter part
court li ness
co" ver ing
co" ve tous
cow ard ice
co" zen age
craf ti ness
cre" du lous
cri" mi nal
cri" ti cism
cri" ti cal
cro" co dile
cru ci fix
cru di ty
crus ti ness
cry" stal line
cul ti vate
cur so ry
cus tom er
Dan ger ous
de" ca logue
de cen cy
de" di cate
de" fer ence
de" li cate
de" pre cate
de pu ty
de" ro gate
de" so late
de" sti tute

des per ate
des po tism
de" tri ment
dex ter ous
di a logue
di a gram
di" li gence
dis ci ple
dis lo cate
dis pu tant
dis so lute
di" vi dend
do" cu ment
dog ma tize
do lor ous
dow a ger
dul ci mer
du pli cate
Ec sta cy
e du cate
e go tism
e lo quent
em bas sy
em bry o
em pha sis
en ter prize
en vi ous
e' pi gram
e' pi logue
e' qui page
eu cha rist
eu lo gy
ex cel lence
ex e crate
ex er cise
ex i gence
ex or cism
ex ple tive
ex qui site
Fa" bri cate
fa" bu lous

fool ish ness
fop pe ry
fas ci nate
fer ti lize
fer ven cy
fes ti val
fir ma ment
fla ge let
fa" tu lent
flow er ed
fluc tu ate
for fei ture
for ma list
for ti tude
fran gi ble
frau du lent
fri" vo lous
fro" lic some
ful mi nate
fur ni ture
Gal lan try
ge" ne rous
ge" nu ine
ger mi nate
glim mer ing
glo bu lar
glos sa ry
glu ti nous
gra" ti tude
gra vi tate
Ha" bi tude
hol low ed
han di ly
har bin ger
har mo ny
ha' zard ous
he" ca tomb
he" mis phere
hep ta gon
he ro ine
hex a gon

hin der ance	lu bri cous	oc ta gon
ho" mi cide	lun a tic	o dor ous
hu mour ous	lux u ry	o" min ous
hus ban dry	Ma" gis trate	or di nance
hy a cinth	mag ne tism	or gan ist
hy" po crite	mag ni tude	or tho dox
I dle ness	mal con tent	out law ry
ig no rance	ma" nu script	o ver sight
im mi nent	mar tyr dom	o ver throw
im ple ment	mar vel lous	Pal pa ble
in di gent	me" cha nism	pal pi tate
in fa mous	men di cant	pa" ra graph
in fan try	me ri ment	pa rent age
in fer ence	mes sen ger	pa tri arch
in flu ence	me" ta phor	pa" tron age
in no cence	me" tho dise	pa" tron ize
in sti gate	mi cro cosm	pau ci tyt
in stru ment	mi cro scope	pe" dan ry
in te gral	mo" nar chy	pen du lum
in ter course	mo" nu ment	pen ta gon
in ter im	mort ga ger	per fo rate
in ter view	mul ti form	per ma nent
in tri cate	mus cu lar	per qui site
i ro ny	mys ti cal	pes ti lence
Jea" lou sy	Nar ra tive	phy si cal
ju bi lee	na" vi gate	plea san try
ju ve nile	ne" bu lous	ple" ni tude
Kil der kin	neg li gent	poig nan cy
kna ve ry	neigh bour ly	po" ly gon
La" by rinth	nig gard ly	por phy ry
la" tin ist	no" mi nate	post hu mous
lau da num	nu me rous	pre am ble
lax a tive	nun ne ry	pre" ci pice
lec tur er	nu tri ment	pri" mi tive
le" ni tive	nu tri tive	prin" ci ple
li bel lous	Ob lo quy	pro" mi nent
li" ber tine	ob se quies	pro" phe cy
li bra ry	ob so lete	pro" se cute
li" ne age	ob sta cle	pros per ous
li" tur gy	ob vi ous	pro" ven der
lou gi tude	oc ci dent	pro" vi dence

pul ver ise
pu" nish ment
pur ga tive
pur chas er
pur ru lent
pu tri fy
py" ra mid
Qua dran gle
qua dru ped
quan ti ty
quar ter age
qui e tude
quin tu ple
Ra" ven ous
re" com pense
rec tan gle
rec ti tude
re mi grate
re tro grade
re" ver ence
re" ver end
rhap so dy
rhe" to ric
rheu ma tism
ru di ments
ru mi nate
Sa" cra ment
sa" ci lege
sanc ti ty
sa" tur nine
sca" ven ger

scru pu lous
scur ri lous
se" di ment
sen si tive
se" pul chre
ser pen tine
ser vi tude
set tle ment
sig na lize
sig na ture
ske le ton
so" le cism
so" lem nize
so" ver eign
spe" cu lum
sphe" ri cal
stig ma tize
stra" ta gem
sub se quent
subs tan tive
sub ter fuge
suc cu lent
sup pli ant
sur ro gate
sy" co phant
sym pa thize
sym pho ny
Tan gi ble
tan ta lize
tech ni cal
te" les cope

tem per ance
ter ma gant
ti mor ous
trac ta ble
trai tor ous
trea" cher ous
tre" mu lous
tri" pli cate
tur bu lent
tur pi tude
tym pa ny
ty" ran nous
Va ga bond
vas sal age
ve he mence
ven di ble
ve" no mous
ven tri cal
ven ture some
ver sa tile
ver ti cal
vin ci ble
vi" ru lent
Un du late
u ni verse
ur gen cy
Wick ed ness
wrong ful ly
won der ful
work man ship
wret ched ly

Accented on the Second.

A ban don
a bate ment
ab hor ence
ab ridg ment
ab strac ted
ac compt ant
ac count ant
af fron tive
ag gres sor

al lot ment
ap pa rent
ap pen dage
arch an gel
arch bi shop
as sem blage
a strin gent
a sy lum
a tach ment

at ten dance
ath le" tic
au then tic
au tum nal
Bal co ny
bal sa" mic
be numb ed
be wil der
bra va do

Ca the dral

chi me ra

clan des tine

co er cive

con cen tric

con junc ture

con sum mate

con tex ture

con tin gent

con vey ance

De base ment

de ben ture

de can ter

de fen dant

de lin quent

de mean our

de mur rage

de port ment

de scrip tive

de spo" tic

di lem ma

dis cern ment

dis cou" rage

dis grace ful

dis gust ful

dis ho" nour

dis man tle

dis plea sure

dis sem ble

dis tin guish

dis tract ed

dis trust ful

Ec cen" tric

ec lip tic

ef ful gence

e ject ment

e lope ment

em bar rass

em bez zle

e mer gent

em pha" tic

en coun ter

en cum ber

en dorse ment

en dow ment

en fran chise

en gage ment

en light en

en or mous

en tice ment

en vel op

e qua tor

es ta" blish

ex che" quer

ex pect ant

ex pres sive

ex tin guish

ex trin sic

ex treme ly

Fa na tic

fan tas tic

fo ren sic

fra ter nal

fre ne" tic

Gi gan tic

gym nas" tic

He ro ic

ho ri zon

hor ri" fic

hu mane ly

hys te" ric

I de a

ig no ble

il lus trate

im por tance

im pos tor

im pru dent

in cul cate

in cum bent

in debt ed

in den ture

in dig nant

in dul gence

in for mer

in he rent

in jus tice

in qui ry

in struc tive

in ter ment

in tes tine

in tes tate

in trin sic

in vec tive

in ven tor

La co" nic

lieu te" nant

Mag ne" tic

ma lig nant

man da mus

me cha" nic

me men to

mis trust ful

mo ment ous

mo nas tic

mu se um

Nar ra tor

noc tur nal

Ob du rate

o bei sance

ob ser vance

oc cur rence

of fen sive

op po nent

op pres sive

op pres sor

Pa ci" fic

pa ter nal

pa the" tic

pel lu cid

per sua sive

pre ce dent

pre cep tive

pre cur sor

pri me val	re fresh ment	se ques ter
pro nos tic	re gard less	so nor cus
pro mul gate	re hear sal	spec ta tor
pro vi so	re lin quish	sple ne" tic
pur su ance	re luc tance	stu pen dous
pur vey or	re main der	sub scrib er
Qua dra" tic	re mon strate	sub ver sive
qua dru ple	ren coun ter	suc cess ful
quan da ry	re pug nant	sy nop sis
qui es cent	re sem blance	Tes ta tor
Re cord er	re sent ment	trans pa rent
re cum bent	se splen dent	tre men dous
re dun dant	Sar cas tic	tri bu nal
re fine ment	scho las tic	tri umph ant

Accented on the Last.

Ab sen tee	dis pos sess	o ver come
ac qui esce	dis re pute	o ver flow
ad ver tise	do" mi neer	o ver look
am bus cade	En gi neer	o ver seer
ap per tain	en ter tain	o ver ween
ap pre hend	es ca lade	o ver whelm
as cer tain	Ga" zet teer	Pa" li sade
Bri" ga dier	gre" na dier	per se vere
ber ga mot	Im por tune	pre ex ist
Can non ade	in ter cede	Qua ran tine
ca" val cade	in ter fere	Re ad mit
ca" va lier	in ter lave	re cog nize
cir cum vest	in ter pose	ren dez vous
com plai sant	in ter rupt	re" par tee
com pre hend	in ter sperse	re" pre hend
con de scend	in ter vene	re" pri mand
con tra dict	in va lid	Se" re nade
coun ter act	Ma ga zine	su per add
De" bo nair	mas que rade	su per scribe
dis ap prove	mis ap ply	su per sede
dis com pose	mis in form	su per vise
dis em bark	Op por tune	Trans ma rine
dis en gege	o ver cast	Vo lun teer

Examples of Words of THREE *Syllables pronounced as* TWO, *and accented on the* FIRST *Syllable.*

Observe that *cion, sion, tion,* sound like *shun,* either

in the middle or at the end of Words ; and *ce. ci, sci, si,* and *ti,* like *sh.* Therefore, *cial, tial,* sound like *shal ; cian, tian,* like *shen ; cient, tient,* like *shent ; cious, scious, tious,* like *shus ;* and *science, tience,* like *shence,* all in one Syllable,

Ac ti on	lus ci ous	pre" ci ous
an ci ent	Man si on	Quo ti ent
auc ti on	mar ti al	Sanc ti on
Cap ti ous	men ti on	sec ti on
cau ti on	mer si on	spe' ci al
cau ti ous	Na ti on	spe" ci ous
con sci ence	no ti on	suc ti on
con sci ous	nup ti al	Ten si on
Dic ti on	O ce an	ter ti an
Fac ti en	op ti on	trac ti on
fac ti ous	Pac ti on	Unc ti on
frac ti on	par ti al	Vic ti on
Gra ci ous	pa ti ence	ver si on
Junc ti on	pa ti ent	vi" sion
Lo ti on	por ti on	

TABLE X.

Words of Four Syllables, accented on the First.

Ab so lute ly	con tro ver sy	e" quit a ble
ac ces sa ry	con tu ma cy	ex e cra ble
ac cu ra cy	co" rol la ry	ex o ra ble
a" cri mo ny	cor ri gi ble	ex pli ca ble
ad mi ral ty	cre dit a ble	ex qui site ly
ad ver sa ry	cus tom a ry	Fi" gu ra tive
a" la bas ter	de" li ca cy	fla" tu len cy
al le go ry	des pi ca ble	fo li a ted
a" ni ma ted	de" sul to ry	for mid da ble
a" po plex y	di" la to ry	Ha" bi ta ble
ap pli ca ble	dis put a ble	he" te ro dox
ar bi tra ry	dor mi to ry	hos pi ta ble
au di to ry	dro me da ry	ig no mi ny
Ce" li ba cy	dy" sen ta ry	i" mi ta ble
ce re mo ny	Ef fi ca cy	in tri ca cy.
cha" ri ta ble	e" li gi ble	in ven to ry
com mon al ty	e" mis sa ry	Ju di ca ture
com pa ra ble	e" pi cur ism	La pi da ry
com pe ten cy	e" pi lep sy	le" gen da ┌

li" ne a ment
li" te ra ture
lu mi na ry
Ma" gis tra cy
ma" tri mo ny
mi" nis te ry
mi ser a ble
mo men ta ry
mo" nas te ry
Na" tu ral ist
na" vi ga ble
na" vi ga tor
ne" ces sa ry
ne cro man cy
nu ga to ry
Ob du ra cy
ob sti na cy
o" per a tive
o" ra to ry
Pa" la ta ble
par li a ment
par si mo ny

pa" tri mo ny
pe" ne tra ble
per se cu tor
pi" ti a ble
plea sur a ble
prac ti ca ble
pre" da to ry
pre" fer a ble
pro" fit a ble
pro fli ga cy
pro" se cu tor
pro mon to ry
pur ga to ry
Rea son a ble
re" pu ta ble
re" vo ca ble
Sa" lu ta ry
sanc ti mo ny
sanc tu a ry
san gui na ry
sea son a ble
se con da ry

se" cre ta ry
se" den ta ry
se" mi cir cle
se" mi na ry.
ser vice a ble
so" li ta ry
sta" tu ary
sub lu na ry
spi" ri tu al
Tem po ra ry
te" nant a ble
to" ler a ble
tri" bu ta ry
Va lu a ble
va ri a ble
va ri e gate
ve" eg ta ble
ve" ge ta tive
ve" ne ra ble
ven ti la tor
vo lun ta ry
vul ner a ble

Accented on the Second.

Ab bre vi ate
ab ste mi ous
ab sur di ty
ac ce" le rate
ac ces si ble
ac ti" vi ty
ad mi" nis ter
ad mis si ble
á do ra ble
ad ver si ty
ad vi sa ble
af firm a tive
a gi" li ty
a gree a ble
a la" cri ty
al le gi ance
al le vi ate
al ter na tive

am bas sa dor
a na" ly sis
an ni hi late
an ta" go nist
an ti" ci pate
an ti" qui ty
a po" lo gy
a pos tro phy
ar ti" cu late
as pe" ri ty
as sas sin ate
as si" mu late
as so ci ate
as tro" no my
au ri" cu lar
au ste" rity
Ba ro me ter
be a" ti tude

be ne" vo lent
be nig ni ty
bo ta" ni cal
Ca la" mi ty
ca li" di ty
ca pi" ci tate
ca pi" tu late
ce le" bri ty
cen so ri ous
cer ti fi cate
co a" gu late
co he ren cy
co in ci dent
col la" te ral
com bus ti ble
com mu ni ty
com pa" ti ble
con ci li ate

con den si ty
con fe" de rate
con for mi ty
con ge ni al
con si" der ate
con so" li date
con ta" mi nate
con ti" gu ous
cor po re al
cor ro" bo rate
cre du li ty
cri te ri on
De ca" pi tate
de clar" a tive
de cli" vi ty
de du ci ble
de fi na ble
de fi" ni tive
de for mi ty
de lec ta ble
de li" be rate
de li" ne ate
de li" ri ous
de no" mi nate
de plo ra ble
de po" pu late
de pra" vi ty
de ter mi nate
dex te" ri ty
di a" go nal
di a" me ter
di rec to ry
dis loy al ty
dis pa" ri ty
dis pen sa ry
dis qua li fy
dis qui e tude
dis se" mi nate
dis si" mi lar
di ver si fy
di vi ni ty

di vi" si ble
dox o" lo gy
duc ti" li ty
du pli" ci ty
E co" no my
ef fec tu al
ef fe mi nate
e la" bo rate
e lec to rate
e lip ti cal
e lu ci date
e man ci pate
e mer gen cy
e mo" lu ment
em pha" ti cal
en co mi um
en or mi ty
en thu si asm
en thu si ast
e nu me rate
e pis co pal
e qui" va lent
e qui" vo cal
e ra di cate
er ro ne ous
e ter nal ly
e van ge list
e va" po rate
e ven tu al
ex ag ge rate
ex as pe rate
ex cru ci ate
ex e" cu tor
ex em pli fy
ex hi" li rate
ex o" ne rate
ex or bi tant
ex or di um
ex pa ti ate
ex pe di ent
ex pe ri ence

ex tem po re
ex te" nu ate
ex ter mi nate
ex tra ne ous
ex tre" mi ty
ex u be rant
Fa ci" li tate
fa ci" li ty
fan tas ti cal
fa ta" li ty
fe li" ci ty
fer ti" li ty
fes ti" vi ty
fi de" li ty
for ma" li ty
for tu i tous
fra ter ni ty
fra gi" li ty
fru ga" li ty
Gar ru" li ty
ge o" me try
gram ma ri an
gra tu i ty
Ha bi" li ment
ha bi" tu ate
har mo ni ous
he re" ti cal
hi la" ri ty
his to ri an
his to" ri cal
hos ti" li ty
hy dro" pi cal
hy po" cri sy
hy po" the sis
I den" ti cal
i do" la try
il li" be ral
il li" ter ate
il lu mi nate
il lus tri ous
im ma" cu late

im men si ty
im mo" de rate
im mo" des ty
im mu ni ty
im mu ta ble
im pal pa ble
im pas sa ble
im pe" ni tent
im pe" ra tive
im per ti nent
im per vi ous
im pe" tu ous
im pla" ca ble
im po" ver ish
im preg na ble
im pro" ba ble
im pro" bi ty
im pu ni ty
im pu ta ble
in ac cu rate
in ad ver tent
in cle" men cy
in cre" di ble
in cre" du lous
in do" ci ble
in ef fa ble
in e" le gent
in fal li ble
in fe ri or
in fir ma ry
in fir mi ty
in ge ni ous
in ge" nu ous
in gra ti ate
in gra" ti tude
in gre di ent
in he" rit ance
in i" qui tous
in i" qui ty
in ju ri ous
in or di nate

in qui e tude
in qui" si tive
in sa ti ate
in sen si ble
in te" gri ty
in tel li gent
in ter ro gate
in ti" mi date
in tract a ble
in tu i tive
in va" li date
in ves ti gate
in ve" te rate
in vi" si ble
in vi go rate
i" ras ci ble
i ro" ni cal
i ra" di ate
ir re" ve rent
La bo ri ous
le ga" li ty
le gi" ti mate
lon ge" vi ty
lu bri" ci ty
Ma chi" ne ry
ma le" vo lent
ma lig ni ty
me cha" ni cal
me mo ri al
me ri" di an
me tho" di cal
me tro" po lis
mi ra" cu lous
mo no" po lize
mo no" to ny
mu ni" ci pal
mu ni" fi cent
mys te ri ous
my tho" lo gy
Na ti" vi ty
ne ces si ty

nu tra" li ty
non en ti ty
nu me" ri cal
Ob li" ter ate
ob li" vi on
ob scu ri ty
ob se qui ous
om ni" po tent
om ni" vor ous
op pro bri ous
o ri" gi nal
or tho" gra phy
Pa ro" chi al
par ti" ci pate
pe cu li ar
pe nin su la
pe nu ri ous
per am bu late
per cep ti ble
per en ni al
per form a ble
pe ri" phe ry
phi lo" lo gy
phi lo" so phy
plu ra" li ty
po li" ti cal
pos te ri or
pos te" ri ty
pre ca ri ous
per ci" pi tate
pre des ti nate
pre oc cu py
pre pa" ra tive
pre pos ter ous
pre ro" ga tive
pre ser va tive
pre va" ri cate
pro fun di ty
pro ge" ni tor
pro lix i ty
pro pen si ty

pro pri e tor

pros pe" ri ty

pro ver bi al

Qua ter ni on

quo ti" di an

Ra pa" ci ty

ra pi" di ty

re cep ta cle

re ci" pro cal

re cri" mi nate

re frac to ry

re ga" li ty

re ge" ne rate

re luc tan cy

re mark a ble

re mu ne rate

re pub li can

res pon si ble

res to ra tive

re sus ci tate

re ta" li ate

re ver ber ate

rhe to" ri cal

ri di cu lous

rus ti" ci ty

Sa ga" ci ty

sa lu bri ous

sa ti" ri cal

scur ri" li ty

se cu ri ty

sep ten ni al

sig ni" fi cant

si mi" li tude

sim pli ci ty

sin ce" ri ty

so lem ni ty

so li" ci tous

so li" ci tude

so li" lo quy

so phis ti cal

sub or di nate

sub ser vi ent

sub stan ti ate

suc ces sive ly.

sul phu re ous

su per flu ous

su pe ri or

su per la tive

su pre ma cy

sus cep ti ble

sym bo" li cal

sy no" ni mous

Tau to" lo gy

te me" ri ty

ter ra que ous

ter res tri al

the o" lo gy

tran qui li ty

trans pa ren cy

tri an gu lar

tri en ni al

ty ran ni cal

Vain glo ri ous

ver na" cu lar

ver ti" gin ous

vi eis si tude

vic to ri ous

vi ra" ci ty

vo ci" fe rous

vo lu mi nous

vo lup tu ous

U bi" qui ty

u na" ni mous

un te" na ble

ur ba" ni ty

un for tu nate

un feign ed ly

un wil ling ness

Accented on the Second, but pronounced as Three.

Ad mis si on

af fec ti on

af flic ti on

am bi ti ous

as per si on

au da ci ous

au spi ci ous

Ca pri ci ous

ces sa ti on

co er ci on

col lec ti on

col lu si on

com mis si on

com pa" ni on

com ple ti on

com pul si on

con ces si on

con fes si on

con tri" ti on

con ver si on

con vul si on

De fi" ci ent

de fluc ti on

de jec ti on

de li" ci ous

de ten ti on

de vo ti on

dif fu si on

di ges ti on

dis cus si on

dis mis si on

dis tinc ti on

Ef fi" ci ent

e jec ti on

e mis si on

es sen ti al

ex emp ti on

ex pan si on

Fal la ci ous

fa mi" li ar

fic ti" ti ous

Im par ti al

im pa tient

in fec ti ous

in nox i ous

Lo qua ci ous

Ma gi" ci an

ma li ci cus

mi gra ti on

Ob nox i ous

of fi" ci ous

o pi" ni on

out ra ge ous

Pre cau ti on

pro fi" ci ent

pro pi" ti ous

Re li" gi ous

Sen ten ti ous

suf fi" ci ent

Ten a ci ous

Ver mi li on

vi va ci ous

vo ra ci ous

Words of four Syllables accented on the First.

Ac ci den tal

a" do les ence

an te ce dent

a" po ple tic

ap pre hen sive

arch an ge" lic

Be a ti ' fic

be" ne fac tor

Co ad ju tor

co a les cence

co e ter nal

co ex is tent

cir cum ja cent

cli" mac" te ric

De cli na tor

de sper a do

de tri men tal

dis af fect ed

dis in he" rit

dis res pect ful

E van es cent

eu ro pe an

Ho ri zon tal

hy me ne al

In co her ent

in con sis tent

in ex haust ed

in stru men tal

in ter ja cent

in ter lo per

in ter reg num

Le" gis la tive

le" gis la tor

le" gis la ture

Ma" le fac tor

ma" ni fes to

ma" the" ma tic

mis de mea nor

Or na men tal

o ver bur den

Per se ve rance

pre" de ces sor

pro" cu ra tor

Re" gu la tor

Sa" cer do tal

sci en ti ' fic

spe" cu la tor

su per car go

TABLE XI.

Words of Five Syllables, accented on the Second.

A bo ' min a ble

a po" the ca ry

au tho ri ta tive

aux i li a ry

Ca lum ni a tor

com men da to ry

com men su ra ble

con so" la to ry

con tem po ra ry

De bi" li ta ted

de cla" ma to ry

de cla" ra to ry

de fa" ma to ry

de ge ' ne ra cy

de ro" ga to ry

dis ho" no ra ble

dis in ter est ed

Ef fe" mi na cy

elec tu a ry

e ma" ci a ted

e pis co pa cy

e pis to la ry

ex pla" na to ry

He re ' di ta ry

he re" ti cal ly

her me" ti cal ly

I ma" gi na ble

i ma" gi na ry

im pe ne tra ble

im prac" ti ca ble

in ac cu ra cy
in ap pli ca ble
in cen di a ry
in com pa ra ble
in cor ri gi ble
in dis pu ta ble
in ex or a ble
in nu me ra ble
in se" pa ra ble
in suf fer a ble
in su per a ble
in tem pe ra ture
in to le ra ble
in ve" te ra cy
in vo" lun ta ry
in vul ne ra ble
ir re" pa ra ble
ir re" vo ca ble
i ti ne ra ry
Jus ti" ci a ry
Ob ser" va to ry
o ri" gi nal ly
Par ti cu lar ize
pe cu ni a ry
pre li" mi na ry
pre pa" ra to ry
Re me di a ble
re po" si to ry
re ci pro cal ly
re co ' ver a ble

in ex pli ca ble
in ex tri ca ble
in fa" tu a ted
in flam ma to py
in ha" bi ta ble
in hos pi ta ble
in im" it a ble
Sub si" di a ry
sig ni" fi can cy
Ver mi" cu la ted
vo ca" bu la ry
vo lup tu a ry
Un ac cept a ble
un al ter a ble
un an swer a ble
un au tho ri zed
un cha" ri ta ble
un ci" vi li zed
un cul ti vat ed
un dis ci plin ed
un fa thom a ble
un fa vor able
un go" vern a ble
un pa" ra lel ed
un par don a ble
un pro" fit a ble
un qua" li fi ed
un ser vice a ble
un ut ter a ble
un war rant able

Accented on the Third.

A ca de" mi cal
a" cri mo ni ous
ad van ta ge ous
af fa bi li" ty
a" li men ta ry
al le" go ri cal
al pha be" ti cal
am phi the a tre
an na the ma tize
a ni ver sa ry

ar chi pe" la go
ar gu men ta tive
a ris to" cra cy
a rith me ti cal
as si du i ty
as tro no" mi cal
Car ti la" gi nous
ca" to go" ri cal
cho ro gra" phi cal
chris ti a" ni ty

chro no lo" gi cal
cir cum am bi ent
com pli men ta ry
con san gui" ni ty
con ti gu i ty
con ti nu i ty
con tra dic to ry
con tra ri e ty
con tro ver ti ble
con tu me li ous
cor nu co pi a
cre" di bi" li ty
cri" mi na" li ty
cu ri o" si ty
Di a bo" li cal
dis in ge" no ous
dis o be di ent
du o de" ci mo
Ec cen tri" ci ty
e co no" mi cal
e las ti" ci ty
e" le men ta ry
em ble ma" ti cal
e pi de" mi cal
e qua bi" li ty
e qua ni" mi ty
e qui la" te ral
e qui li" bri um
e" ty mo" lo gy
ex com mun ni cate
Flex i bi" li ty
Ge ne a" lo gy
ge" ne ra" li ty
ge" ne ro" si ty
Hos pi ta" li ty
hy per bo" li cal
hy per cri" ti cal
hy" po cri" ti cal
hy" po the ti cal
Ig no mi" ni ous
il le ga" li ty

il le gi" ti mate
im be ci" li ty
im ma tu ri ty
im me mo ri al
im mo bi" li ty
im mo ra" li ty
im mor ta" li ty
im per cep ti ble
im por tu ni ty
im pro pri e ty
in ac ces si ble
in ad ver ten cy
in ar ti" cu late
in ca pa" ci ty
in ci vi" li ty
in com mo di ous
in com pa" ti ble
in con ceiv a ble
in con gru i ty
in con si" de rate
in con so la ble
in con test a ble
in con ve ni ence
in cor po re al
in cor rup ti ble
in cre du li ty
in de fea si ble
in de ter mi nate
in dis cri" mi nate
in dis pen sa ble
in di vi" du al
in di vi" si ble
in ef fec tu al
in e qua" li ty
in ex haus ti ble
in ex pres si ble
in fe li" ci ty
in fer ti" li ty
in fi de" li ty
in ge nu i ty
in hu ma" ni ty

72   THE CATHOLIC SCHOOL BOOK.

in sig ni" fi cant
in sin ce" ri ty
in sta bi" li ty
in stan ta ne ous
in sup por ta ble
in sur mount a ble
in te lec tu al
in ter me di ate
in tre pi" di ty
in u ti" li ty
in va li" di ty
ir re fra" gi ble
ir re sist a ble
ir re proach a ble
ir re triev a ble
Li" ber a" li ty
lon gi tu di nal
Ma gis te ri al
mag na ni" mi ty
ma" nu fac tu rer
ma" tri mo ni al
me di o" cri ty
me" ri to ri ous
me ta mor pho sis
me" to pho ri cal
me" ta phy" si cal
me tro po" li tan
mi" nis te ri al
mis cel la ne ous
mo" no syl la ble
mu ci la" gi nous
mul ti fa ri ous
mu ta bi" li ty
my tho lo" gi cal
Non con for mi ty
no to ri e ty
O do ri" fe rous
op por tu ni ty
o ra to" ri cal
or tho gra" phi cal
Pa" ne gy ri cal

pa" ra dox i cal
pa" ral le" lo gram
par si mo ni ous
pa" tri mo ni al
pe ri o" di cal
per pen di cu lar
phi lo so" phi cal
phra se o" lo gy
phy si og no my
plau si bi" li ty
po" ly syl la ble
pos si bi" li ty
pre ter na" tu ral
pri mo ge ni al
pri mo ge" ni ture
prin ci pa" li ty
pro" ba bi" li ty
pro" ble ma" ti cal
pro" di ga" li ty
pu e ri" li ty
pu sil la" ni mous
py ra mi" di cal
Qua dri la te ral
quin qua ge si ma
Re ca pi tu late
rec ti li" ne al
re" gu la" ri ty
re" pre hen si ble
re" pre sen ta tive
ri" si bi li ty
Sa lu ti" fe rous
sa" tis fac to ry
se ni o" ri ty
sen si bi" li ty
sin gu la" ri ty
su per pon de rate
su per e" mi nent
su per ex cel lent
su per flu i ty
sup pe da ne ous
sys te ma" ti cal

Ta ci tur ni ty
tes ti mo ni al
the o lo" gi cal
the o re" ti cal
tri" go no me" try
ty po gra" phi cal
Vo" lu bi" li ty
Un ac count a ble
un ac cus tom ed

u na ni" mi ty
un at tain a ble
un a void a ble
un con trol a ble
un de ni a ble
un en light en ed
un e qui" vo cal
u ni for mi ty
un in ha bit ed

Accented on the Third, but pronounced as Four.

Ad ven ti" ti ous
am mu ni" ti on
ap pre hen sion
ap pro ba ti on
a" va ri" ci ous
aug men ta ti on
Be ne dic ti on
Cal ci na ti on
cir cum spec tion
cir cum stan ti al
cir cum ven ti on
com pre hen si on
con de scen si on
con fi den ti al
con fir ma ti on
con fis ca ti on
con fla gra ti on
con sci en ci ous
con se quen ti al
con su ma ti on
con tem pla ti on
De" cla ma ti on
de" pri va ti on
de" pre ca ti on
dis pen sa ti on
dis pro por ti on
Em bro ca ti on

e" ner va ti on
e qui noc ti al
ex cla ma ti on
Fa" bri ca ti on
fas ci na ti on
fer men ta ti on
fla gel la ti on
fluc tu a ti on
In au spi" ci ous
in suf fi ci ent
Li" que fac ti on
ma" chi na ti on
Pal li a ti on
pe" tri fac ti on
pro vi den ti al
Re" tri bu ti on
re tro spec ti on
Sa" cri le gi ous
se ques tra ti on
sti" mu la ti on
sti" pu la ti on
su per ci" li ous
su per fi" ci al
su per scrip ti on
sup pli ca ti on
sup po si" ti on
Trans mu ta ti on

TABLE XII.

Words of Six Syllables, accented on the Third.

Ex tra or di na ry
Il le gi" ti ma cy

in com men su ra ble
in de fa ti ga ble

D

in sig ni fi" can cy
in stan ta ne ous ly
in ter ro" ga to ry
ir re co" ve ra ble

Re" com mem da to ry
Va le tu di na ry
Un in ha bi" ta ble
un in tel li gi ble

Accented on the Fourth.

An te di lu vi an
Com pa" ti bi" li ty
Dis ci" pli na ri an
di vi" si bi" li ty
Ec cle si as ti cal
e" ty mo lo" gi cal
Fa mi li a ri ty
He" te ro ge' ne ous
hi er o gly" phi cal
Il li be ra" li ty
un mu ta bi" li ty
un pla ca bi" li ty
im pro ba bi" li ty
in cre di bi" li ty

in fa li bi" li ty
in fe ri o" ri ty
in flex i bi" li ty
in hos pi ta li ty
Me di ter ra ne an
Pa ci ' fi ca to ry
par li a men ta ry
par ti" cu la" ri ty
pu sil la ni mi ty
Re spec ta bi" li ty
Spi" ri tu a li ty
. su per in ten den cy
sus cep ti bi" li ty
Tri go no me tri cal

TABLE XIII.

Words of Seven Syllables, accented on the Fifth.

An ti tri ni ta ri ans.
Im ma te ri a li ty
im mea su ra bi li ty
im pa ri syl la bi cal
im pe ne tra bi li ty
in com pa ti bi li ty

in dis so lu bi li ty
in di vi si bi li ty
in sa ti a bi li ty
La ti tu di na ri an
Ple ni po ten ti a ry
Va le tu di na ri an

TABLE XIV.

Words spelt alike. but which in different parts of speech, change their pronounciation ; being accented on the first *syllable, when Nouns ; and the* last, *when Verbs.*

NOUNS. *Accented on the First.*	VERBS. *Accented on the Last*
Absent, not present	To Absent, to keep away
An Abstract. an abridgement	To Abstract, to shorten
A Collect, a short prayer	To Collect, to gather toge-ther
A Compound, a mixture	To Compound, to mingle
A Contest, a quarrel	To Contest, to dispute
A Contract, a deed	To Contract, to bargain

NOUNS.	VERBS.
Accented on the First.	*Accented on the Last.*
Converse, conversation	To Converse, to discourse
A Convert, a reformed per-son	To Convert, to change
A Convict, a criminal	To Convict, to prove guilty
A Convoy, a guard	To Convoy, to protect
A Desert, a wilderness	To Desert, to forsake
An Extract, a quotation	To Extract, to select
A Ferment, a tumult	To Ferment, to work like beer
Frequent, a repetition	To Frequent, to resort to
Import, tendency	To Import, to bring from abroad
An Insult, an affront	To Insult, to illuse
An Object, anything present-ed to our senses	To Object, to oppose
A Present, a gift	To Present, to give
Produce, the thing produc-ed	To Produce, to bring forth
A Project, a scheme or de-sign	To Project, to contrive
A Rebel, a traitor	To Rebel, to revolt
A Record, a public register	To Record, to enroll
Refuse, waste	To Refuse, to deny
A Subject, he who owes obe-dience	To Subject, to subdue
A Torment, a great pain	To Torment, to torture

TABLE XV.

Words of Similar Sound, but different in Spelling and Sense.

Abel, a man's name	Affect, to move or imitate
Able, sufficient	Effect, purpose
Accept, receive	Ail, to be ill
Except, leave out	Ale, malt liquor
Accidence, in grammar	Ere, before
Accidents, chances	Heir, to an estate
Accompt, reckoning	Alder, a tree
Account, esteem	Elder, a senior
Acts, deeds, exploits	All, every one
Axe, an intrument	Awl, a sharp tool

D2

Altar, for a sacrifice
Alter, to change
Ant, an insect
Aunt, an uncle's wife
Arrant, notorious
Errand, a message
Errant, wandering
Ascent, steepness
Assent, consent
Assistance, help
Assistants, helpers
Attendance, waiting
Attendants, waiters
Auger, to bore with
Augur, a soothsayer
Bacon, swine's flesh
Baken, by an oven
Beacon, a mark
Beckon, with the hand
Bail, a surety
Bale, a large parcel
Bait, a lure
Bate, to lessen
Ball, a round substance
Bawl, to cry out
Baron, a lord
Barren, unfruitful
Barbarra, a woman's name
Barbary, a country
Barberry, a tree
Bare, naked
Bear, a savage animal
Baize, a coarse cloth
Bays, in architecture
Base, mean
Bass, in music
Be, to exist
Bee, an insect
Beach, the sea-shore
Beech, a tree
Bean, a plant

Been, of the verb to be
Beat, to strike
Beet, a plant
Beer, malt liquor
Bier, a frame for the dead
Bel, an idol
Bell, to ring
Belle, a fine lady
Berry, a small fruit
Bury, to inter
Bile, gall
Boil, to move by heat
Blew, did blow
Blue, a colour
Boar, a male swine
Bore, to make a hole
Board, a plank
Bored, did bore
Bole, a corn measure, &c.
Bowl, a large basin
Bolt, for a door
Boult, to shift
Bomb, a mortar shot
Boom, of a ship
Bough, a branch
Bow, to bend
Boarder, at a table
Border, the margin
Boy, a young lad
Buoy, an anchor mark
Buy, to purchase
By, near
Brace, a couple
Braze, to solder
Breaches, broken places
Breeches, a garment
Bread, food made of corn
Bred, brought up
Brewing, of ale
Bruin, a bear's name
Brews, he breweth

Bruise, a hurt
Bruit, a report
Brute, a beast
But, a particle
Butt, a large cask
Borough, a town
Burrow, cover for rabbits
Cain, a man's name
Cane, to walk with
Calais, in France
Chalice, a cup
Call, to name
Caul, of a wig. &c.
Cannon, a great gun
Canon, a rule or law
Calendar, an almanack
Calender, to smooth
Catch to lay hold of
Ketch, a small ship
Ceiling, of a room
Sealing, setting a seal
Cell, a small close room
Sell, to dispose of
Cellar, a vault
Sellar, who sells
Censer, for incense
Censor, a critic
Censure, judgment
Cent, a hundred
Sent, did send
Scent, a smell
Centuary, an herb
Century, 100 years
Sentry, a guard
Cession, resigning
Session, act of sitting
Chased, did chase
Chaste, continent
Choir, a set of singers
Quire, 24 sheets of paper
Choler, wrath

Collar, for the neck
Chord, in music
Cord, a small rope
Cinque, five
Sink, to sink down
Cite, to summon
Sight, seeing
Site, situation
Citern, an instrument
Citron, a sort of fruit
Clause, a section
Claws, talons
Cleaver, for chopping
Clever, ingenious
Climb, to get up
Clime, climate
Clothes, apparel
Coarse, not fine
Course, to race
Coat, a garment
Quote, to cite or allege
Coin, money
Kine, cows
Quoit, to play with
Kite, a bird of prey
Comet, a blazing star
Commit, to act
Coming, approaching
Cummin, a plant
Common, public
Commune, to converse
Concert, of music
Consort, a wife
Condemn, to sentence
Contemn, to despise
Confidence, reliance
Confidants, trusty friends
Council, an assembly
Counsel, advice
Courant, a quick dance
Current, passable

Cousin, a relation
Cozen, to cheat
Creak, to make a noise
Creek, of a sea
Crick, a pain in the neck
Cruise, to sail about
Crews, ship's companies
Cygnet, a young swan
Signet, a seal
Cymbal, an instrument
Symbol, a mark
Cypress a tree
Cyprus, an island
Dane, of Denmark
Dean, next to the bishop
Deign, to vouchsafe
Dear, costly
Deer, a forest animal
Debtor, that oweth
Deter, to frighten from
Decease, death
Disease, distemper
Defer, to delay
Differ, to disagree
Deference, respect
Difference, disagreement
Dependence, relying on
Dependents, hangers on
Descent, going down
Dissent, to disagree
Device, a stratagem
Devise, to invent
Dew, a thin cold vapour
Due, owing
Dire dreadful
Dyer, one who dyes cloth
Doe, female deer
Dough, leaven or paste
Doer, perform
Door, of a house
Dollar, a Spanish coin

Dolour, grief
Done acted
Dun, a colour
Draft, a bill
Draught, a drink
Dragon, a serpent
Dragoon, a soldier
Ear, of the head
Ere, before
Easter, the feast of our Saviour's resurrection
Esther, a woman's name
Emerge, to rise out of
Immerge, to plunge
Eminent, noted
Imminent, impending
Enter; to go in
Inter. to bury
Envoy, ambassador
Envy, ill will
Err, mistake
Her, she
Yew, a tree
You, yourself
Your, your own
Ure. custom use
Ewer, basin
Exercise, employment
Exorcise, to conjure
Extant, in being
Extent, dimensions
Eye, to see with
I. myself
Fain, willingly
Feign, to dissemble
Faint, languid
Feint, a pretence
Fair, beautiful
Fare, diet, hire
Favour, kindness
Fever, distemper

Feat, exploit
Feet, of the body
File, of steel
Foil, to overcome
Fillip, with the finger
Philip, a man's name
Fir, a tree
Fur, soft hair
Flea, an insect
Flee, to run from danger
Flew, did fly
Flue, of a chimney
Flower, of the field
Flour, for bread
Forth, onward, forward
Fourth, in number
Foul, nasty, unclean
Fowl, a bird
Frances, a woman's name
Francis, a man's name
Freeze, to congeal
Freize, a coarse cloth
Furs, the plural of fur
Furz, a prickly bush
Gallon, four quarts
Galoon, a ribbon
Gale, a strong wind
Gall, bile
Gaul, a Frenchman
Gait, manner of walking
Gate, an entrance
Gesture, action
Jester, a joker
Gilt, gilded
Guilt, sin
Glutinous, sticking
Gluttonous, greedy
Grease, soft fat
Greece, a country
Grate, a fire place
Great, large

Grater, a coarse file
Greater, larger
Greaves, leg armour
Grieves, he laments
Groan, hard sigh
Grown, increased
Groat, four pence
Grot, a cave
Guess, a think
Guest, a visitor
Hail, frozen water
Hale, hearty
Hair, of the head
Hare, an animal
Hall, a great room
Haul, to pull
Hallow, to consecrate
Hollow, empty
Harrass, to fatigue
Arras, hangings
Harsh, severe
Hash, minced meat
Hart, deer
Heart, the seat of life
Haven, a harbour
Heaven God's throne
Heal, to cure
Heel, of a shoe
Hear, hearken
Here, in this place
Heard, did-hear
Herd, of cattle
Hew, to cut
Hugh, a man's name
Hue, colour
Hie, to hasten
High, lofty
Higher, more lofty
Hire, wages
Him, that man
Hymn, a pious song

Hole, a cavity
Whole, not broken
Home, dwelling
Whom, who
Hoop, for a tub
Whoop, to halloo
Hour, of the day
Our, belonging to us
Idle, lazy
Idol, an image
Aisle, of a church
Isle, an Island
Imposter, a cheat
Imposture, deceit
In, within
Inn, a public house
Incite, to stir up
Insight, knowledge
Indite, to compose
Indict, to impeach
Ingenious, inventive
Ingenuous, candid, free
Innocence, harmless
Innocents, babes
Intense, excessive
Intents, purposes
Knap, on cloth
Nap, short sleep
Nape, of the neck
Knave, a rogue
Nave, of a wheel
Knead, to work dough
Need, did want
Knew, did know
New, not born or used
Knight, a title of honour
Night, darkness
Knot, a knob
Not, denying
Lade, to load
Laid, to place

Latin, a language
Latten, brass
Lattice, a net-work window
Lettice, a woman's name
Lettuce, a salad
Leak, to run out
Leek a kind of onion
Lease, a tennure
Leash, three, a thong
Lead, metal
Led, conducted
Leaper, a jumper
Leper, one leprous
Least, smallest
Lest, for fear that
Legislator, law-giver
Legislature, parliament
Lessen, to make less
Lesson, in reading
Lesser, smaller
Lessor, grantor, of a lease
Liar, a false story-teller
Lier, one who rests
Lyre, a harp
Limb, leg or arm
Limn, to paint
Limber, pliant
Limner, painter
Line, length
Loin, a joint of meat
Lo ! behold
Low, mean, humble
Loth, unwilling
Loath, to nauseate
Loose, slack
Lose, not to win
Made, finished
Maid, a woman servant
Mau, chief
Maine, of a horse
Mail, armour

Male, he or him
Manner, custom
Manor, lordship
Mare, a female horse
Mayor, of a town
Marsh, watery ground
Mash, to mince
Marshal, head general
Martial, warlike
Marten, a bird
Martin, a man's name
Mary, a woman's name
Marry, to wed
Merry, gay of heart
Mean, of small value
Mien, behaviour
Meat, flesh
Mete, to measure
Medal, a coin
Meddle, to interfere
Medlar, a fruit
Meddler, a busy body
Message, errand
Messuage, house
Metal, gold, silver, &c.
Mettle, sprightliness
Mews, for horses
Muse, to think
Might, power
Mite, an insect
Moan, lamentation
Mown, cut down
Moat, a ditch
Mote, an atom
Moor, a fen or marsh
More, in quantity
Morning, before noon
Mourning, lamenting
Muscle, a shell fish
Muzzle, to tie the mouth
Muslin, fine linen

Muzzling, to gag
Naught, bad
Nought, nothing
Nay, an adverb
Neigh, as a horse
Neither, of the two
Nether, lower
Oar, to row with
Ore, uncast metal
Hoar, grey with age
Of, belonging to
Off, distant or from
Oh! an exclamation
Owe, indebted
Pail, for water
Pale, wan or white
Pain, torment
Pane, of glass
Pair, two
Pare, to cut or chip
Palate, to taste or relish
Palette, used by painters
Pall, funeral cloth
Paul, a man's name
Parcel, a small bundle
Partial, blessed
Patience, mildness
Patients, sick people
Pause, to stop
Paws, of a beast
Peace, quietness
Peas, pulse
Peal, in ringing
Peel, to strip off
Peer, a nobleman
Pear, a well-known fruit
Pier, of a bridge
Penitence, repentance
Penitents, repentants
Peter, a man's name
Petre, saltpetre

Pick, to choose

Pique, a grudge

Pillow, a bag of feathers

Pillar, a round column

Pint, half a quart

Point, the sharp end

Pistol, a small gun

Pistole, a Spanish coin

Place, to set in order

Plaice, a kind of fish

Plait, a fold

Plate, silver

Pleas, law suits

Please, to satisfy

Poesy, poetry

Posy, motto on a ring

Pole, a long stick

Poll, a head. a vote

Poor, needy

Pore. to look closely

Porcelain, china ware

Purslain, an herb

Pour, to stream

Power, to command

Practice, exercise

Practise, to study

Praise, commendation

Prays. entreateth

Pray, to beseech

Prey, a booty

Precedent, an example

President, a governor

Principal. a chief

Principle, first cause

Profit. gain

Prophet a foreteller

Quarry, a stone mine

Query, a question

Quaver a note in music

Quiver, for arrows

Quean a harlot

Queen, a king's wife

Race, running

Raze, demolish

Radish, a root

Reddish, inclining to red

Rain, water

Reign, to rule

Rein, a bridle

Raise, to lift up

Rays, beams of light

Raisin, a dried grape

Reason, argument

Rare, uncommon

Rear, to erect

Read, to peruse

Reed, a small pipe

Rede, counsel

Regimen, diet

Regiment, of soldiers

Relic, remainder

Relict, a widow

Rest. ease

Wrest, to force

Rome, a city

Room, chamber

Rhyme, verse

Rime, frost

Rice, a kind of grain

Rise, advancement

Rigger, one who rigs

Rigour, severity

Ring. circle

Wring, to twist

Right, just, true

Rite, a ceremony

Wright, a man's name

Write, to tell by letters

Rhode, an island

Road a highway

Roe, deer

Row, ranged in a line

Rote, from memory
Wrote, did write
Ruff, a neckcloth
Rough, uneven
Rung, did wring
Wrung, twisted
Sail, of a ship
Sale, selling
Sage, wise
Sedge, a narrow flag
Scent, to smell
Sent, ordered away
Sense, understanding
Since, afterwards
Say, speak
Sey, a sort of cloth
Scene, part of a play
Seen, beheld
Sea, ocean
See, to behold
Seal, an impression
Zeal, ardent affection
Seam, a joining
Seem, to pretend
Seas, the waters
Sees doth see
Seize, to lay hold of
Sew, with a needle
Sue, to intreat
Shear, to clip
Sheer, to go off
Shew, to make appear
Shoe, for the foot
Shoar, a prop
Shore, the sea coast
Sine, a line
Sign, a token
Sloe, a wild plumb
Slough, a miry place
Slow, not speedy
Sole, bottom of the foot

Soul, the spirit of man
Some, part
Sum, the whole
Stair, a step
Stare, to look earnestly
Steal, to pilfer
Steel, hardened iron
Straight, direct
Strait, narrow
Succour, help
Sucker, a young twig
Tacks, small nails
Tax, a tribute
Tares, among wheat
Tears, from the eyes
Team, a set of horses
Teem, to abound
Tenor, intent
Tenure, to hold land
Than, in comparison
Then, that time
The, an article
Thee, thou
Their, belonging to them
There, that place
Throne, chair of state
Thrown, hurled
To, unto
Toe, part of the foot
Too, also
Two, a couple
Tour, a journey
Tower, a lofty building
Treatise, conventions
Treatise, a discourse
Vale, a valley
Veal, calves' flesh
Vain, meanly proud
Vein, a blood vessel
Valley, a dale
Value, worth

Wain, cart or waggon	Whey, of milk
Wane. to decrease	Week, seven days
Wait. tarry	Weak, faint
Weight. for scales	Whither, to what place
Ware, merchandise	Wither, to decay
Wear, the thing worn	While, space of time
Were to have been	Wile, a trick
Where at what place,	Vile, despicable
Way, road	Would, was willing
Weigh, to balance	Wood, small timber
Wax, tenacious matter	Won, did win
Vex, to tease	One, in nuuber
Wey, forty bushels	

OF POINTS AND STOPS.

A comma (which is marked thus ,) is the shortest of all stops, and serves to divide short sentences, till you come to the full sense. As thus: *1 am persuaded that neither death, nor life, nor angels, nor principalities, nor powers, nor things present, nor things to come, nor height, nor depth, nor any other creature, shall be able to separate us from the love of God, which is in Christ Jesus our Lord.*—Rom. viii., 38, 39.

A Semicolon (;) serves also to part sentences, and is often used when the sentences are contrary. Thus; *A soft answer turneth away wrath ; but grievous words stir up anger.*—Prov. xv, 1. Or thus: *I desired you to get your lesson by heart ; but instead of that you have been at play.*

A colon (:) parts several sentences. every one of which has a full meaning of its own, though, at the same time, it leaves us in expectation of something that is to follow. For example : *He is a wise and prudent boy who minds his book: learning and good education are better than riches.*

A Period (.) is a full stop, and shews the perfect end and conclusion of a sentence. As thus: *Obey your parents. Fear God. Honour the King.*

Observe.—You are to stop at a comma till you can tell *one ;* at a semicolon, till you can tell *two ;* at a colon, till you can tell *three ;* at a period, till you can tell *four.*

A note of Interrogation (?) is always set at the end of a question that is asked. For example : *Who made you? How old are you? What is the matter?*

A note of Admiration (!) is placed after such words or expressions as signify any thing strange or wonderful. Thus: *Oh! Alas! Surprising!* Or thus: *O the depth, both of the wisdom and knowledge!*—Rom. xi., 33.

A Parenthesis ( ) is used to include words in a sentence, which may be left out without injury to the sense. As, *We all (including my brother) went to London.*

The Hyphen (-) is used to separate syllables, and the parts of compound words. As *Watch-ing, Well-taught.*

The Aspostrophe (') denotes that a letter or more is omitted. As, *Lov'd thro,'* for *loved, through, &c.* It is also used to mark the possessive case. As, *The King's Navy,* meaning *The King his Navy.*

Quotation, or a single or double comma turned, (' or ") is put at the beginning of speeches, or such lines as are extracted out of authors.

PART II.

READING LESSONS.

CHAPTER I.

Of the end for which man was created.

Of things necessary for man to know, the end for which he came into the world deserves his first attention, because, being a rational creature, he ought to act for a final end, in the enjoyment whereof he may find his eternal happiness. Now he cannot act for this end without a knowledge of it, which, exciting a desire, makes him search for and employ the means of obtaining it. A man who knows not his last end is like a beast, because he regards only things present; things material, and sensible, after the manner of brutes, and in this he is much more miserable than they. since they find in these exterior objects the felicity they are capable of; but he, instead of finding repose, meets with nothing but disgust, and the source of endless misfortune.

From a want of considering their last end, originates all the disorders discernible in the lives of men, because forgetting that noble and divine end for which their Creator designed them, they are wholly taken-up with pleasures of this mortal life, living upon Earth as if made for the Earth. It would move one to compassion to see a child born of royal blood, and destined by his birth, one day, to wear a crown, yet bred up amongst peasants, and ignorant of his extraction, applying himself only to till the earth, bounding all is pretensions within the scanty limits of earning a miserable livelihood with the sweat of his brow, without having the least thought of the high rank for which he was born, but it is much more to be deplored to see men, who are the children of Heaven, designed by the Almighty to reign there eternally, live in an entire forgetfulness of that end for which they were created, and, setting all their affections upon earthly things, wretchedly deprive themselves of that immense happiness which the bounty of their Creator prepared for them in Heaven.

For this reason, Theotime, resolving to exhort you to embrace virtue in your youth, I propose to you first what you are and for what end you were created, that knowing this your end, you may ardently aspire to it and by early endeavours render yourself worthy of it. Recollect yourself then, and reflect upon three things, what you are, who made you, and for what end.

1. You are a man, that is, a creature endowed with understanding and reason, composed of a body, the structure whereof is admirable, and of a reasonable soul, made in the image of God: in a word you are the most perfect of all visible creatures.

2. You were not made by yourself, for that is impossible; you received from another the being you now enjoy. And from whom have you received it, but

from Him who created Heaven and Earth, and who is the Author of all things? It is He who formed your body in your mother's womb, and brought your soul out of nothing by his power. You are the work of a God, and besides the Father you have upon Earth, you have another in Heaven, to whom you owe all that you possess.

3. But why did Gód make you? Be attentive, Theotime : for what end, think you, did God place you in this world? Was it to enjoy the sensual pleasures and satisfactions of this life? To heap up riches? to acquire glory and reputation amongst men? Nothing less! You have a soul too noble to be destined for such wretched and perishable things : pleasures are changed into pain, riches perish, and glory vanishes. Is it to continue a long time upon earth, to find there your happiness. and to look for nothing after this life? If so there is no difference betwixt you and irrational beings.

Does not this, so noble a soul which God has bestowed on you, endowed with understanding, will, and memory, capable of knowing all things, clearly manifest that you were created for a higher and more honourable end?— Does not this figure of the body you bear, the stature erect, the head on high, and eyes raised towards Heaven, teach you that you are not made for the Earth? Beasts are made for the Earth ; there they find their happiness, and for that reason they look upon the earth : but you, dear Theotime, you are created for Heaven. This is not the place of your abode, as it is that of your origin : your soul came down from Heaven, and it ought to return thither.

But what will you find in Heaven that can render you happy? Will it be the sight of the firmament, with all those beauteous stars? Of the Sun, that admirable instrument, the work of the Most High, and of all that is wonderful and great in Heaven? No. All these are not able to effect your felicity : God has esteemed them too mean for you ; he made them for your service, not to be the object and cause of your happiness. In a word, consider all that is in the universe, those vast and wonderful things

which God has created ; all which are not able to complete
your happiness.

God hath not made you for any of these things. For
what then ? For nothing less than the possession and enjoyment of himself in heaven. He has not judged the
fairest of his creatures worthy of you : He has given
Himself to be the object of your happiness. For this reason he gave you a soul, formed to his image, capable of
possessing him, and which by reason of this capacity, is
never content nor satisfied with the possession and delight of
this life, as every one finds by experience.

You were then not made for creatures, dear Theotime,
but for the Creator. Your last end is not the enjoyment
of creatures, but of God himself. You were created to be
happy by the possession of a God in Heaven, and to reign
with him in a felicity incomprehensible to human understanding. The eye hath not seen, nor the ear heard,
neither hath it entered into the heart of man what things
God hath prepared for them that love him

And, this for how long? For all eternity ; that is, for
a time which shall never end, but continue as long as God
himself. This is the most noble end for which you were
designed, this is the inheritance which your celestial
Father has prepared for you ; this is that end for which he
has created you. All this visible world was but destined
for your present use, to help you in promoting the glory
of God.

CHAPTER II.

What it is to be a Christian.

By the grace of God, Theotime, you are a Christian:
but do you understand what this is, and what you are
by this quality ; Take notice of it then, and learn to
know the great favour God bestowed upon you in the day
of your baptism. By the baptism which you have received, you are washed from original sin, by the appli-
cation of the merits of the blood of Jesus Christ, delivered from the universal curse of mankind, incurred by

sin, and freed from the power of the Devil. You have been made the child of God, the disciple of Jesus Christ your Saviour. You have acquired God for your father; Jesus Christ, for your master, your instructor, your example, and for the rule of your life; the Holy Church, for your mother and guardian; the angels for your protectors; the saints for your intercessors.

You have been made the temple of God, who dwells in you by grace; the heir to his eternal kingdom, from the title and hope of which you were fallen for ever; and you are brought back in the secure way that leads to it, being made a member of Jesus Christ and his Church, out of which all those who obstinately remain cannot be saved, and wherein you are now illuminated with the light of the faith of Jesus Christ, instructed by his doctrine, nourished by his precious body and blood, assisted by his grace, and furnished with all the necessary means for your salvation.

O God! how noble and how honourable is the state of a Christian! What acknowledgments, dear Theotime, ought you to render to Almighty God, who has heaped upon you such immense favors! God was no ways bound to do thus much for you. Without this favor which God has shewn you, you could never have been saved; for there is no salvation without faith. Where then should you have been, if God, had not shown you this mercy? He has not done this favour to thousands of men who live in other countries, in the darkness of ignorance and sin, nor to many other persons, who although they may be baptized as you, yet live in error, separated from the true faith of the Catholic Church, which is the pillar and ground of truth.

Why were you not of that unhappy number? Why has God made you to be born in a Christian country rather than others, and in the bosom of the Catholic Church, where you are instructed in the divine mysteries, and things necessary for salvation? How have you merited his favour? What happiness is it for you, dear Theotime, to have experienced so great a bounty of our God.

We are happy, O Israel, because the things that are
pleasing to God are made known to us. O how fortu-
nate are we by the grace of God, which has called us
to the knowledge of his divine mysteries and adorable
will ! He has not shown his goodness to all the world ;
and' why has he done it to us rather than others ? O
dear Theotime, how is it possible that we should not
fix our affection upon a God who has loved us so
much ?

Learn here from a Christian king, the esteem you
ought to have for your vocation. St. Lewis, king of
France,, had such a value for the favour of God showed to him in making him a Christian, that he not only
preferred it before his kingdom, as in effect it is infinitely greater, but having been baptized in the castle of
Poissy, he would bear that name and be called Lewis
of Poissy, and thus signed his letters and despatches,
esteeming his title more glorious than that of King of
France. And St. Augustin, speaking of the Emperor
Theodosius, says, That he accounted himself more happy in being a member of the Church than Emperor of
the world. These great men, Theotime, knew how to
value the grace of Christianity according to its real
worth.

CHAPTER III.

*That God requires and particularly accepts the services
of Young People.*

The time of youth being the beginning of life, you
must know, dear Theotime, the strict obligations you are
under of consecrating yourself to God when young. The
first is, that God earnestly desires to be served by you
in that age, since it is certain that in all things, God
claims particularly the first and the beginnings. For
this reason in the old law, he commanded the first fruits
of all things to be offered to him. Of fruits, he required
the first gathered to be presented ; of beasts, the first
brought forth to be sacrificed ; and of men, the eldest
sons to be dedicated to his service in the temple, though
he permitted them to be afterwards redeemed, shewing

by this institution, that notwithstanding all things being
equally his, yet he had a special claim for the first, as
those which, above all things, were due to him, and
which he required as an acknowledgement.   Hence the
time of youth being, the beginning and first part of our
life, God demands it particularly, and will have it offered
to him, in order to be faithfully employed in his service.

Secondly, the time of youth is most pleasing to God :
because, generally speaking, according to the natural
order of things, it is the most innocent part of life, least
corrupted by sin : for then the knowledge of evil is
not so extensive, neither is there so much ability or
opportunity to commit it ; the judgment is not perverted
by the false maxims of the world, nor the inclinations corrupted by the infection of the wicked, as in a more advanced
age.   Moreover, our baptismal grace, which we have then
only lately received, renders that more agreeable to
God, at least in those who do not forfeit it by a sinful
life.

But, take notice, Theotime, I said that youth is less corrupted, generally speaking, and according to the natural
order of things, yet it is but too true, that oftentimes much
wickedness is found in it ; though contrary to the order of
nature, which has endowed that age with a simplicity of
mind, and innocence of manners ; hence they are so much
the more guilty, who, by their malice, and depravity, corrupt the good dispositions which nature has bestowed upon
it, learning wickedness and running after it in an age
when nature herself teaches nothing but simplicity and innocence.

Thirdly, because youth is the time of affording the most
opportunities of shewing that you love God sincerely ; for
it is the time of the first temptations, wherein you begin to
be solicited to renounce his love and service.

You are hurried on by your own passions, which
are then the strongest; invited by those of your age,
who often solicit you to wickedness, either by their
example, or by their discourse, and prompted by the

enemy of your salvation, who uses all his endeavours to withdraw you from the service of God, and make sure of you betimes.

So that this age may properly be called the age of combat and trial; wherein you show your love to God with a constant and real affection, if you courageously resist these assaults.

These reasons, Theotime, convince us that God has a special affection for the homage of youth, which being employed in flying from sin and serving God, is a sacrifice the most agreeable that can be offered to Him. And as a learned author says, excellently well, those who in the time of youth overcome themselves by courageously resisting all temptations to sin, and who consecrate themselves entirely to the service of God, make one continual sacrifice of their youth to God, which offering cannot but be most agreeable to Him, as long as it remains undefiled by sin. O Theotime, retain well this truth in your mind, and never forget it.

CHAPTER IV.
Remarkable Instances of the Aversion God bears to Wicked Young People.

God has an aversion to all sinners, as he himself has said " I abhor the wicked," especially those who have ungratefully abused his love and benevolence. Not only reason but experience evinces it, by the effects which God frequently shews of that aversion He has to vicious young people. I shall produce two very remarkable instances out of the sacred Scriptures, that no one may doubt of them, and that from these one may judge of others.

That first example is of the two children of the high priest Heli, called Ophni, and Phinees. These two young men were employed by their father in the ministry of the temple and sacrifices wherein' they behaved themselves very ill, committing great irreverences in the temple, and crying injustices towards the faithful who came to offer their sacrifices to God, requiring from them, by an insatiable avarice, more than was their just due; insomuch that the sacred Scripture says, they were the children of Belial, (so it calls those whom it would signify to be wicked and abandoned; for Belial signifies, without restraint or fear,) having lost the fear of God and the remembrance of their duty: moreover it adds that their sin was very enormous in the sight of God.

Their iniquity provoked God so much that He sent Samuel to tell their father, who had been too negligent in correcting his children, that he would punish him with such rigour, as should serve for an example to all posterity; that he would exclude his family from the high-priesthood, which he would give to another; that his offspring would die in the flower of their youth, and few should arrive at perfect age; and that his two sons, Ophni and Phinees, should both die in one day; and all their race should bear forever the marks of their iniquity, which should never be expiated by victims and sacrifices.

All this happened as was foretold. A little while after, Ophni and Phinees were killed, being defeated by the Philistines. .On the same day, the father, hearing the news of their death, fell down backward, broke his skull, and died upon the spot. Many other misfortunes happened that day; among the rest, the ark of God was taken by the enemy, and the rest of the prophecy was fulfilled to a tittle. How many misfortunes in one family through the wickedness of two sons!

The second is Absalom, the third son of David. He was proud, dissembling, revengeful, and highly ambitious, conceited of himself, and his own beauty, which according to the Scriptures, was extraordinary. The first wicked action which the Scripture relates of him, but which must have needs been preceded by many others, is the murder of his brother Amnon. By this action he lost his father's favour, and was banished from him for the space of five years, after which he was recalled and admitted to his favour again.

He was scarce returned to his father's court, when he contrived a grand rebellion against him; and having by his address gained the affection of the people he retired to a small town, and was proclaimed King. After this he takes up arms against his father, forces him to fly from Jerusalem, and pursues him with a strong army, which he had raised to deprive him of his crown. What will the Divine Justice do here ? Will it connive at such a degenerate child ?

Hear, Theotime, what the sacred Scripture relates : David, seeing himself brought to such straits by his son, was obliged to make head and oppose him. He sets in order the few forces he had with him, sends them to fight, and gives him battle. Absalom's men, though far more numerous, are defeated. In this discomfiture, (O the divine judgments !) it happens that Absalom, endeavouring to save himself by flight, was carried under a great oak, and as he wore his locks very long, his hair, by a strange accident, and particular permission of God, was so strongly, entangled in the branches of the tree that the mule he rode on could not carry him away, but continuing its course left him hanging by his hair, without being able to disengage himself.

David's soldiers seeing him in this condition, run him through with a lance, and killed him on the spot ; although David, by an astonishing tenderness, when sending them to the battle, had expressly forbidden any violence to be offered his person. O Divine justice I thou plainly shewest that thou dost not connive at the iniquities of wicked children ; although thou deferrest for a time the chastisement they deserve, to give them leisure to repent. Thou afterwards punishest most severely their obstinacy in sin, and the affront they offer to thy goodness, with which thou expectest their repentence.

CHAPTER V.

That Salvation generally depends on the time of Youth.

I wish, Theotime, that you, and all those of your age, would thoroughly understand and never forget this truth, that salvation almost entirely depends on the life you lead during your youth. This is unknown to the greatest part of men, but the ignorance of which is the ruin and damnation of many. I wish all youth rightly understood that immense eternity of happiness or misery, which waits them after this life, depends upon this first part of our time which all the world slight, and which the most part employ in wickedness. To convince you of this truth, I shall produce nothing less than the sentiment of the sacred Scriptures, that is of the Holy Ghost, whose words are so express that it is impossible to doubt of it. For why doth it in so many places exhort young people to think of their salvation betimes, and to apply themselves to virtue in their youth, except it were to shew of how great importance that time is for their salvation ?

What does it say in Ecclesiasticus, "Remember thy Creator in the days of thy youth, before the time of afflic- tion comes ?" From whence comes it that it assures us in the Book of Proverbs, 'Instruct a young man according to his way, and when he is old he will not depart from it ?" that is the manner of life of which he has began. Where- fore does it say by the prophet Jeremy, that "it is good for a man when he has borne the yoke from his youth ?" that is, has app'ied himself to virtue, and to bear the pleasing yoke of God's commandments.

Why, in Ecclesiasticus are youth so earnestly exhorted to virtue, by those excellent words, able to soften the most insensible hearts :—" My son, from thy youth up' receive instruction, and, even to thy grey hairs, thou shalt find wisdom. Come to her as one that plougheth and soweth, that is with care and labour, and wait for her good fruits. For in working about her thou shalt labor a little, and shalt quickly eat of her fruits. How very unpleasant is wisdom to the unlearned, and the unwise will not con- tinue with her. But with them to whom she is known, she continueth even to the sight of God,"—vi, 18. All the rest of the chapter is but a continued exhortation to young people to be virtuous. Wherefore in the twenty- fifth chapter, does it say, " The things that thou hast not gathered in thy youth, how shalt thou find them in thy old age ?"

Lastly, among the books of several Scriptures, why was there one expressly made for the instruction of youth, which is that of Proverbs? Does not all this manifestly discover that the Holy Ghost would give men to understand, that the time of youth is a greater consequence than the greatest part imagine; and that all happiness or misery of man, whether in this life or in the next depends generally on that time being well or ill employed; this observation being generally true, that those secure their salvation who in their youth are bred up in the fear of God, and of observance of his commandments; and that those who have not been educated in the fear of God, or cast it from them, to follow sin with greater liberty, are unhappily lost. All this truth is grounded on those two principles; the first is, that those who have followed virtue in their youth, easily persevere through the remainder of their life; the second, that on the contrary, those who give themselves over to sin at that time, with difficulty amend, and frequently never.

CHAPTER VI.

Remarkable examples of those who, having been Virtuous in their youth, continued so all their life.

The first example which I shall produce is that of Joseph, a model of virtue in his youth, and which I have slightly mentioned in the first part. At sixteen years of age he abhorred vice in such a manner that the wicked example of his brethren could never corrupt his innocence; on the contrary not being able to endure their wickedness, he gave notice thereof to his father, Jacob. The greatness of his virtue, for which he was singularly favored by God, and tenderly loved by his father, drew upon him the enmity of his brethren, who meeting him one day in the fields, conspired to murder him; but having a horror of dipping their hands in his blood, they resolved to let him down into a pit, with a design of leaving him there to perish.

This poor child, not able to soften their cruelty by

prayers and tears was obliged to yield putting all his confidence in God, who never abandon those who love him.
In this he was not deceived; for his inhuman brethren,
struck with horror at so barbarous a crime, changed their
first resolution.   They drew him up out of the pit and sold
him to merchants then passing by, who carried him into
Egypt, where he was sold to a lord of that country.   Jo-
seph being with his master, persevered in virtue and innocence of life which drew down the blessing of God upon
the house of his master, who soon discovered his merit, and
conceived a great affection for him.

Behold how Joseph spent the first part of his youth, that
is, until about the age of twenty.   See the consequence of
it, and how he passed the rest of his life ; wherein I observe
three remarkable occasions in which his virtue underwent
the severest trial.   The first was about that age when he
sustained the most violent attack his chastity could undergo.
The second was his being cast into prison, having to suffer
the punishment, and be deemed guilty of a crime he abomi-
nated.

But Joseph continued immovable in his first virtue : and
as he had learned patience in his youth, by the persecution
of his brethren, he bore this with wonderful constancy,
comforting himself in the conviction of his innocence, of
which God was both witness and protector.   God, who had
always been with him, left him not on this occasion ; but,
as the Sacred Scripture says, descended with him into the
pit, that he might assist him with his grace and wonderfully
deliver him, as he did presently after.

To these two trials succeeded the third, yet greater.—
This was the elevated station to which he was raised ; for
having interpreted Pharaoh's dream, by the knowledge God
gave him of things to come, this king not only delivered
him out of prison, but made him the first man in his kingdom, over which he gave him a general charge with
absolute power to dispose of all things according to his
will, commanding his subjects to obey him as himself.—
In this high station, which generally dazzles men's eyes,
and soon destroys an ordinary share of virtue, Joseph

E

remained firm in his primitive innocence, always like him-self.

Forgetfulness of God, pride, covetousness, and revenge, the usual attendants of unlimited power, could never find admittance into his breast. Having an opportunity of re-venging himself on his brethren, who came into Egypt to buy provisions during a severe famine, he not only·omitted it, but received them with such tenderness, and marks of affection, as to draw tears from those who read the Scrip-ture account of it. He carried himself in this station with so much justice, that no complaint was ever made of his conduct; on the contrary, the Egyptians proclaimed him their deliverer, being freed from want during a seven year's famine, by his great prudence, for which he was called in those countries, *The Saviour of the World.*

He persevered thus in virtue and the fear of God, in the midst of grandeur from the age of thirty, when he was raised to that fortune, even to the age of a hundred and ten, wherein he died. O Theotime, reflect well upon this example, and learn from it what virtue acquired in youth is able to effect.

The next example I shall adduce is that of Toby the father of young Toby, whose conduct, as well in youth as in a more advanced age, the Scripture declares to be worthy of our admiration. He was a young man of the tribe and city of Napthali; and, although he was the youngest of all his tribe, yet nothing childish or youthful appeared in his actions. And when all others went to sacrifice to the golden calf of Jeroboam, King of Israel, shunning their company, he went alone to Jerusalem, to the Temple of the Lord, and there adored the God of Israel, offering to him faithfully his first fruits and tithes. These and such like things did he observe, adds the Scrip-ture, when but a boy, according to the law of God.

O the admirable life, Theotime, of a young man who acted nothing childish, that is, nothing contrary to virtue; who permitted not himself to be carried away by the tor-rent of ill-example, continuing steadfast in the service of

God, when the rest, to a man, abandoned their Creator! A youth spent so virtuously could not but be followed by a holy life, as you shall see.

Toby being come to man's estate, was led captive by the Assyrians, with all his countrymen, to the city of Ninive. Being there. he departed not from the path of virtue which he had so happily entered in his youth. For first, as he had learned in his youth to resist the wicked examples of others he permitted not himself to be corrupted in his captivity by the examples of his countrymen, who ate licentiously the meats of Gentiles. though prohibited by the law of God. Secondly, having deserved a particular regard from the Assyrian king, by his virtuous conduct, he had leave to go to any part of the kingdom. He visited his fellow captives, admonished them concerning their salvation and their perseverance in the service of God. Thirdly, the affliction of the captives increasing, he daily visited and comforted them. distributing what he was able to give them, fed the hungry. clothed the naked, and with an unparalleled charity, buried all the dead he found, notwithstanding the displeasure of the king, which he had incurred by that action, even to the danger of his life.

But what is yet more admirable is the patience with which he bore the melancholy affliction of blindness, which befel him by an unexpected accident in the fifty-sixth year of his age. One day, as he returned home, wearied with the burial of many dead, he chanced to fall asleep under a wall, from the top whereof the dung out of a swallow's nest fell upon his eyes, and took away his sight. This was doubtless a very great affliction, and a most severe trial; but he supported it with such an admirable patience, that the sacred Scripture compares it to that of Job, and, what is very remarkable, attributes it to the piety and fear of God in which he had lived during his youth. Behold what it says: Now this trial the Lord therefore permitted to happen to him, that an example might be given to posterity of his patience, as also of holy Job. For whereas he had always feared God from his infancy, and kept his commandments, he repined not against God because the evil of blindness had befallen him, but continued immovable in the fear of God, giving thanks to God all the days of his life."

O how admirable is the effect of virtue, which has always increased with age? He was delivered from his affliction four years after, and living to the age of one hundred and ten, he died in peace, after he had made, as the Scripture observes, a continual progress in the fear and service of God. Thus, Theotime, do they live, thus do they die, who have followed virtue in youth.

CHAPTER VII.

That those who had been addicted to vice in their youth amend with great difficulty, and often not at all.

O Theotime, that I had been capable of imprinting this important truth more lastingly in your heart than in brass or marble, and making you perfectly comprehend the great and dreadful difficulty of amendment after a youth spent in vice. A difficulty so great that it is almost impossible sufficiently to express it; and the other side so general that we cannot consider it attentively, without being touched with a lively sorrow, seeing such numbers of christians, and principally of young people, who groan under the tyranny of a vicious habit, which being contracted in their youth, and increased with age, leads them to perdition; from which, if they chance to recover, it is with incredible pains and combats, and by a manifest miracle of divine grace. Learn, dear Theotime, to avoid this danger, and endeavour to conceive its greatness, either that you may entirely prevent it, or quickly withdraw yourself, if you are already engaged therein.

This great difficulty springs from three causes. The first is, the incredible power and force of a wicked habit, which being once rooted in the soul, cannot be plucked up without great pains. All habits have commonly this quality, that they continue a long time, and are with much difficulty removed. But amongst others, wicked habits are such as adhere more strongly, and are not so easily changed ; because corrupt nature is more prone to evil than good. Hence the Scripture says, That the perverse are hard to be corrected, which makes the number of fools, that is, of sinners, infinite. But among the wicked habits, those contracted in youth are the strongest and with most difficulty overcome ; for the passions which are the instruments of vice, unrestrained at that time by virtue, increase with age, and as they increase give vice daily new strength, and render it at last unconquerable.

For this reason the same Scripture, in order to express the force of a vicious habit contracted in youth, delivers a sentence which young people ought to have frequently in their mind : "His bones shall be filled with the vices of his youth, and they shall sleep with him in the dust." That is, the vices and wicked habits of youth become so deeply rooted in the soul, that all the remainder of life is tainted with them, and death alone, as we daily see, can put a final period to them.

The cause is very evident ; for vice, when once in possession of a soul, increases and strengthens the passions ; the passions corrupt the judgment, so that it mistakes good for evil, and evil for good ; the judgment being once corrupted perverts the will, which runs blindly into sin, and from thence proceeds all the evil : because, as St. Augustin says, " The will not governed turns to an eager desire of sin, and by our gratifying this desire, it is formed into a habit, and a habit not resisted becomes a necessity ;" that is, an extreme difficulty in avoiding sin. Hence, when a person is arrived at this pitch ; there are no hopes of his amendment ; because as another author (St. Isidore) adds, " Necessity terminates in death by exposing him who lies under it to final impenitence."

The second cause of this great difficulty is, the decrease of divine grace : for as God multiplies his favours to those who receive him with humility, and employ them for their salvation, so he diminishes them to those who abuse and condemn them. Now if he deals thus with mankind in general, much more with youth, on whom he bestows many favours, as long as they remain deserving of them, so he withdraws his kindness when they abuse them, as we may learn by the experience of those, who, having been favoured with particular obligations from God in their youth, presently becomes sensible of a great diminution of those favours, occasioned by the ill use they have made of the same.

God himself threatens this by his prophet when he speaks thus : In that day the fair virgins and the young men shall faint for thirst ; they that swear by the sin of Samaria ; that is who make profession of adoring the idols which the city of Samaria adores. The thirst, is not only a corporeal but a spiritual thirst, and the want of divine grace, of which it is spoken immediately before : I will send forth a famine into the land, not a famine of bread, nor a thirst of water, but of hearing the word of the Lord.

The third cause of the great difficulty of correcting the habits contracted in youth is, the power of the devil, who gains ground in proportion as our sins increase, and the grace of God is diminished. This is the proper effect of sin, viz., after depriving a soul of the grace and protection of her Creator, to subject her to the dominion of the devil, and engage her more and more in that unhappy slavery, in proportion as she continues in vice. O Theotime, who can sufficiently express the deplorable state of a soul reduced to that servitude, under the tyranny of the mortal enemy, who employs all his engines and devices to destroy her without recovery, but suggesting all temptations that are likely to draw her into sin ; by furnishing her daily with new occasions for destruction ; by diverting her from those that might withdraw her from her unhappy state ; by hurrying her from sin to sin, from one vice to another, till the measure of her iniquities being filled up, she is at last abandoned to the Devil, by a visible effect of Divine wrath.

Thus does this cruel enemy treat those whom he has under his power, by a just permission of God, who thus rejects those who withdraw themselves from His service and friendship, and who, refusing to submit themselves to the sweetness of his law, and the abundance of his favours and blessings, most justly deserve to be abandoned to that cruel master, who breathes nothing but their destruction, and will never cease to persecute them till he has plunged them into eternal damnation. How unhappy are all those who have fallen into this deplorable slavery; yet they are still more miserable, who, whilst therein, think not of seeking their deliverance.

CHAPTER VIII.

Examples of those who have never corrected the Vices of their Youth.

As in a shipwreck, where a ship is lost in a storm, there are many who perish, and very few who save themselves by swimming or otherwise, so in the shipwreck of virtue, which many suffer in their youth, the number of those who are eternally lost is very great, but of those who escape, very small. You will conceive the smallness of this number, when you shall know, Theotime, that in the history of the Old Testament there is found but one example, a thing almost incredible, is the person of Manasses, king of Judah. For this one, it produces a vast number of others who perished in the storm, and died in the vices of their youth: some, after a long life; others, being snatched away by death in the prime of their age. I shall here set you down some examples:

First; Of all the kings of Israel who, to the number of nineteen, reigned over the ten tribes of Israel, when the division was made of that kingdom from that of the tribe of Judah, after the death of Solomon, there was scarce one but was extremely wicked from his youth, and continued so to his death. And although the Scripture does not make express mention of their youth, nevertheless it gives us sufficiently to understand that they were all wicked in that age, except Jehu, who was afterwards perverted like the rest.

Amongst the kings of Judah, who likewise reigned

to the number of nineteen, after Solomon, there were six who were good, that is Asa, Josaphat, Ozais, Jonathan, Ezechias, and Josias ; all the others were wicked. Those, who were good began from their youth, and continued such all their life ; the greatest part of those who were . vicious began their wickedness in their younger years, and never altered their conduct.

Thus it is said of king Ochosiec that he began to reign about twenty-two years of age : that he was wicked and attached to the idolatry of the impious Achab, king of Israel, which was taught him by his mother, Athelia, sister of that wicked king. He reigned but a year, at the end whereof he died in his wickedness.

It is said of Achaz that he was twenty years of age when he began to reign ; that he did not apply himself to good, and to the service of God, but followed the example of the idolatrous kings of Israel, and that he far surpassed them in impiety, wherein he died after he had continued in vice for the space of sixteen years.

Amon reigned at the age of tweny-two, and became a follower of the vices of his father Manasses, but not of his repentance, and died in his sins at the end of two years, murdered by his own servants.

Joachin began at the age of twenty-five, and reigned eleven years, during which time he was wicked like his ancestors, and died in his iniquities, without being lamented by any one, and also deprived of the honour of burial, according to the threat of the prophet Jeremy.

His son . Joachim, having succeeded at the age of eighteen, reigned but three months, at the end whereof he deserved, for his sins, to fall into the hand of Nebuchodonosor, and was sent into Babylon, where he died a long time after.

Sedecias, the last of the kings of Judah, being come to the crown at the age of twenty-one, was also wicked like his predecessors ; and having continued in his iniquities for the space of eleven years, he drew upon himself and his people the most rigorous effect of that vengeance, with which God had long threatened the Jewish nation ; for in the ninth year of his reign the city of Jerusalem was besieged by Nebuchodonosor, king of Babylon, and after two years siege, it was taken, pillaged, and put to fire and sword, the temple of God ransacked and burnt, and whoever had escaped the fury of the sword or famine, were sent into captivity. Sedecias himself, flying with his children, was taken and brought before the proud king, who after venting his fury and indignation, caused his children to be butchered before his face, and afterwards pulled out his eyes and sent him captive into Babylon, where he died in misery, in just punishment of his iniquities.

To these examples, which are very common in Sacred Scripture, of such as have never corrected their vice in their youth, and who have died in their sins, we find but one in the Old Testament who was sincerely converted after he had lived wickedly in his youth, viz. Manasses, and he in so extraordinary a manner, that this example shows clearer vicious inclinations in youthful years.

The prince having lost his father Ezechias, one of the most pious kings of Judah, at the age of twelve years, inherited his crown, but not his virtues : for, soon forgetting the holy example and wise documents he had received from him, he addicted himself to every kind of vice and impiety. His iniquities daily increased until the fifteenth or, according to others, until the two-and-twentieth year of his reign, wherein God punished his crimes in an exemplary manner. He was taken by the Assyrians in the city of Jerusalem, sent captive into Babylon, loaded with irons and chains, and cast into a frightful prison, where he suffered every degree of misery and persecution.— Being reduced to this extremity he began to open his eyes, and call upon God in his afflictions, whom he had forgotten in his prosperity. He acknowledged his iniquities, and sued for pardon with a truly contrite heart, and by the force of tears and prayers, obtained from God his deliverance ; after which he did penance for his sins, and lived in holiness all the remainder of his life, even to the

E3

age of sixty-seven, when he died   See here, Theotime, a conversion after a wicked youth, but a conversion purchased at a dear rate.

CHAPTER IX.

That the Devil uses all his endeavours to lead Young People into vice.

To be convinced of the importance of dedicating yourself to God in your youth, you must remember that the Devil, that sworn enemy to man's salvation, fearing nothing more than to see you virtuous in your youth, employs all his endeavours to overcome you, and all those of your age, that he may ruin you, without hope of recovery.

This truth is manifest from all we have said before. That cursed fiend, who studies nothing but to rob God, as much as he can, of the honour due to him, and men of the happiness prepared for them, knows very well that to lead youth into vice is the means of taking from God the first and greatest acknowledgment which men owe to him. In the second place, he knows how injurious to God a wicked life in youth is; and thirdly the dreadful consequence of it, viz., a deep engagement in sin, hardness of heart, and impatience of mind.   Moreover, he understands very well, that there is no other more certain way to fill the earth with iniquities and to damn mankind.—This is the reason why he employs all his industry to corrupt the innocence of youth, the first sources of salvation, and all other blessings.   He knows well that to poison the waters of a fountain, it is sufficient to cast venom into the spring, which communicates it easily to all the brooks; and that to conquer a realm, the best method is to secure the frontier places, which give entrance into the heart of the country.

The cursed fiend understands well how to put in practice the mischief he taught Pharaoh, to whom he suggested the destruction of all the male infants of the Israelites, that he might exterminate the people of God.

He exercises daily both the malice and the cruelty of Nebuchodonosor, who, having taken king Sedecias, with his children, at the sacking of Jerusalem, caused the children's throats to be cut before the father's face, and satisfied himself by putting out the father's eyes, without taking away his life. Thus the cruel enemy employs all his malice to murder the children by sin, and strives to blind interiorly the parents, that, neither seeing nor caring for the loss of their children, they may not deliver them from such imminent danger.

The same king returning into his country, proud and elevated with his victories, carried as the fairest part of his triumph, the young people of the city of Jerusalem prisoners before him, as is related by the prophet Jeremy. He left nothing in that desolate city more to be lamented, than the deplorable loss of the young people, which the same prophet bewails above all other calamities.

Thus, dear Theotime, this detestable fiend, who, as the Scripture says, is established king over all the proud, has no greater reason insolently to triumph over the holy church, than by the multitude, of young people, which he keeps in slavery by sin. And this pious mother counts no loss more deplorable than that of her dear children, which the enemy snatches from her in their youth, some by one vice, others by another, but most by the sins of impurity, which is the strongest chain by which he holds them in captivity ; thus exercising the rage he has conceived against her from her first establishment, and continuing the war he has sworn to wage against all her children, according to the revelation made by St. John in the Apocalypse.

This war of the enemy of mankind against young people is a thing so manifest, that the same St. John, writing to the faithful, and congratulating every age for the blessings most peculiar to them, expresses a particular congratulation to young people, for the victory they have gained over the enemy, as being those who were most persecuted.

"I write to you young men," says he " because you

have overcome the wicked one. I write to you, young men, because you are strong, and the word of God abideth in you, and you have overcome the wicked one."

Happy are all those young people to whom with truth we may say, that they have conquered the enemy of salvation. I represent unto you here the war he wages against those of your age, that we may congratulate you in that manner; and that by the persecution he raised against you, you may know first how necessary it is that you should be virtuous in your youth, since the Devil endeavours so powerfully to corrupt you. Secondly, with how much courage you ought to resist the attempts of that cruel enemy, who seeks your destruction with so much fury? How is it possible you should not stand in horror of that enemy, and dread, more than death, to let yourself be overcome by him, who seeks all ways to destroy you for ever!

CHAPTER X.
On the Knowledge of True Virtue.

The first means of acquiring virtue is the knowledge of it, and the discerning of solid piety from that which is false and imaginary.

Many seem to love virtue, who are far from it, because they love not virtue, as it is in itself, but as they represent it to themselves, every one according to his own inclination. Some think themselves virtuous, when they are not of the number of the wicked.— Others place virtue in abstaining from certain vices, from which they have a· kind of aversion, though, subject to others no less criminal in the sight of God. Others esteem themselves virtuous if they follow some religious practises, although on the other side they wholly neglect the interior regulation of their conscience, too often defiled with mortal sin. All these are so much the more to be lamented, as they imagine themselves to be in a good way, when they are absolutely out of it; and thinking to arrive by that course at the port of salvation, they find them-

selves at length in the direct road to perdition : veri-
fying in that respect the saying of Solomon. "There is
a way which seemeth just to man but the end thereof
leadeth to death."

Virtue, Theotime, does not depend on the opinion
of men : it is the work of God. From Him, then must
we learn its rule, since He alone can direct in what manner He will be served.

Hearken, then, to what God says of it in the Sacred
Scripture, and He will teach you how wisdom, that is,
virtue, consists in fearing God, and flying absolutely
from sin, and that He has thus instructed man in his
creation, " Then," says Job, that is, in the beginning
of the world. " God said to man, Behold the fear of the
Lord, that is wisdom ; and to depart from evil, that is
understanding."

He teacheth the same thing by the royal prophet, by
whom He gives you the general rule of virtue, " Decline
from evil and do good."

Wise Solomon informs you of the same truth. " Fear
God." says he, "and keep his commandments : in that
consist the perfection of man, for that he was born, that
is his last end and real happiness."

In short, the Sacred Scriptures acknowledges no other
wisdom of piety than the fear of God, which it calls the
beginning, the fullness, and the crown of wisdom.
Now this fear is not that which is purely servile, that
is, apprehends more the punishment that detests the
sin ; but is a loving fear of the children of God, which
makes them hate sin, because it displeases God, and
love good, because it is agreeable to Him : like the fear
and respect a good child bears his father, which makes
them fearful to offend, and diligently seek all means of
pleasing him.

So that, Theotime, according to the maxims of the
divine school, true virtue consists in the fear of God,
which produces a voluntary observance of his commandments, and causes a fear and detestation of offending God above all things, and seeks means to
please Him, and retain His favour. This, alone ought
to be accounted virtue ; and that which is not direc-

ed by this certain and infallible rule, is to be deemed false piety.

CHAPTER XI.
Of Prayer and Instruction.

Of all the means of attaining virtue, prayer is the most important. It is not sufficient to desire it; we must search for it with all diligence; and that we may successfully seek it, we must go to the fountain-head, and beg it of Him, who is the author of it, and bestows on those who beg it as they ought. If any of you want wisdom, let him ask of God, who giveth to all abundantly.

This is the means which wise Solomon employed, together with that ardent desire of wisdom, whereof we have just now spoken. For in the same place he says that after he had considered all the perfection of wisdom he conceived such ardent love for it, that he searched on all sides to find it; and that in consideration of the innocence of his tender-age, which he had hitherto preserved untainted, God gave him to understand that wisdom to the effect of his grace, which he could not obtain without God's assistance; whereupon addressing himself to the author of all wisdom, he requested it of him with all the strength of his heart, in the prayer we shall set down in this chapter.

Besides this excellent example, the Scripture also furnishes you with that of the wise author of Ecclesiasticus, who describes thus the means he made use of in his youth to acquire virtue; "When I was yet young, before I wandered about, I sought for wisdom openly in my prayer. I prayed for her before the temple, and unto the very end I will seek after her. My foot walked in the right way. From my youth up I sought after her, I stretched forth my hands on high, and I bewailed my ignorance of her. I directed my soul to her, and in knowledge I found her.

This is the way these great men took to acquire wisdom in their early years. The Scripture proposes it to all young people as the method they ought to imitate for attaining it.

It behooves you, Theotime, who by the grace of God aspire to that wisdom, to imitate them, and follow the way they have shewn. Beg daily of God, with all the ardour of your affection, this wisdom, which removes ignorance, banishes sin, and leads by the path of virtue to real felicity; offering Him from the bottom of your heart that excellent prayer of Solomon.

"God of my fathers, and Lord of mercy, who hast made all things with thy word, give me wisdom that sitteth by thy throne, and cast me not off from among thy children; for I am thy servant, and the son of thine handmaid, a weak man, and of short time, and falling short of the understanding of judgment and laws. Send her out of Thy Holy Heaven, and from the throne of Thy Majesty, that she may be with me, and labour with me, that I may know what is acceptable with Thee; for she knoweth and understandeth all things, and shall lead me soberly in thy works, and shall preserve me by her power. So shall my works be acceptable."

With this prayer, or some such like it, if you say it as you ought, you will obtain all that you ask for. But remember that it must have these three conditions to be efficacious; it must be humble, fervent, and persevering. Humble, acknowledging that you cannot obtain wisdom or virtue, but from God alone. Fervent, to beg it with a most earnest desire. Persevering, to beg it daily, as there is no way wherein the Divine grace is not necessary to preserve or increase it.

Besides the means of prayer, instruction is also necessary for obtaining virtue. Though none but God can give wisdom, yet ordinarily He does not bestow it but by the ministry of men, by whom He is pleased we should be instructed in the paths of virtue, inspiring by his grace our hearts with his holy truths, at the same time that men teach us by their words. For this reason He has established in his Church pastors and doctors, as the Apostle says, to teach men divine truths, and conduct them in the way of salvation.

Now, if instruction be necessary for all men, it is particularly so for young persons, who by reason of

their age, have little knowledge of the maxims of wisdom, and are incapable of discovering them without assistance.

It is not sufficient, dear Theotime, to beg daily wisdom and virtue from Almighty God: you must desire
and seek after instruction and direction in the way to
it from them who know it.

This desire of instruction is so necessary for obtaining
virtue, that it is the beginning thereof according to that
of the wise man.   " The beginning," says he, of her
[wisdom] is the most true desire of discipline.

And lastly, that you may be fully convinced, read
attentively this excellent exhortation of Ecclesiasticus;
" Son," says the wise man, "if thou will attend
to me, thou shalt learn ; and if thou wilt apply thy
mind, thou shalt be wise. If thou wilt incline thine
ear, thou shalt receive instruction ; and if thou love
to hear, thou shalt be wise. Stand in the multitude
of ancients that are wise and join thyself from thy
heart to their wisdom, that thou mayest hear every
discourse of God, and the sayings of praise may not
escape thee.

Now there are many ways by which we may receive
instruction in virtue, as preaching, and books of piety.
But that which is most necessary for you at your age, is
the particular direction of a wise and virtuous person, who
may teach you the true way of salvation. For this reason
the wise man adds to the former words, " if thou see a
man of understanding, go to him early in the morning,
and let thy foot wear the steps of his doors."

CHAPETR XII.
Of Devotion to the Blessed Virgin.

One of the last means which I assign, but also one
of the most effectual, for acquiring virtue in youth,
is devotion to the Blessed Virgin. It is infallible to such
who assiduously employ it, because it affords at the same
time the most powerful intercession in the sight of God
for obtaining his favour, and the most perfect model for
our imitation.

Next to God, and the most adorable humanity of his son Jesus Christ, it is she whom we must chiefly honour and love, by reason of that most sublime and excellent dignity of Mother of God, which raises her above all creatures which God has ever created.

By her we may receive all the assistance which is necessary for us. She is most powerful with God, to obtain from him all that she shall ask of him. She in all goodness in regard of us, by applying to God for us. Being Mother of God, she cannot deny us her intercession when we have recourse to her. Our miseries move her, our necessities urge her; the prayers we offer her for our salvation, bring to us all that we desire; and Saint Bernard is not afraid to say, "That never any person invoked that mother of mercy in his necessities, who has not been sensible of the effects of her assistance."

Although the Blessed Virgin extends her goodness to all men, yet we may say she has a particular regard for young people, whose frailty she knows to be greatest, and necessities the most urgent, especially for the preservation of chastity, which is most assaulted in that age, and of which she is a singular protectress. History is full of examples of saints, who have preserved this great virtue in their youth, by the assistance of this Queen of Virgins; and experience affords daily examples of those who have gained great victories, by the recourse they have had to her intercession, and who have happily advanced themselves in virtue, under the protection and by the grace she obtains of God for them.

Be therefore devout to the Blessed Virgin, dear Theotime; but let it not be the devotion of many, who think themselves so, in offering some prayer to her more by custom than devotion; and on the other side, exceedingly displease her by a life of moral sin, which they commit without remorse. What devotion is this, to desire to please the mother, and daily crucify the son, trampling his blood under their feet, and contemning his grace and favor? Is not this to be an enemy both to son and mother.

O dear Theotime, your devotion to the Blessed Virgin must not be like that: it must be more generous and holy. And, to speak plainly, if you will be a true child, and a sincere servant of the Blessed Virgin, you must be careful to perform four things:

1. Have a great apprehension of displeasing her by mortal sin, and of afflicting her motherly heart by dishonouring her Son, and destroying your soul ; and if you chance to fall into that misfortune, have recourse readily to her, that she may be your intercessor in reconciling you to her Son, whom you have extremely provoked. "She is the refuge of sinners as well as of the just, on condition they have recourse to her with a true desire of converting themselves," as St. Bernard says.

2. Love and imitate her virtues, principally her humility and chastity. These two virtues, among others, rendered her most pleasing to God. She loves them particularly in children, and is pleased to assist with her prayers those whom she finds particularly inclined to those virtues, according to the same Saint.

3. Have recourse to her in all your spiritual necessities. And, for that end, offer to her daily some particular prayers: say your beads, or the little office, some times in the week; perform something in her honour on every Saturday, whether prayer, abstinence or alms; honour particularly her feasts by confession and communion.

4. Be mindful to invoke her in temptations, and in the dangers you find yourself in of offending God. You cannot shew your respect better than by applying yourself to her in these urgent necessities, and you can find no succour more ready and favourable than hers. It is the counsel of St. Bernard. "If the winds of temptations be raised against you, if you run upon the rocks of adversity, lift up your eyes towards that star, invoke the Blessed Virgin. In dangers, in necessities, in doubtful affairs, think upon the Blessed Virgin, let her not depart from your mouth, nor from your heart; and that you may obtain the assistance of her intercession, be sure to follow her example."

If you perform this, you will have a true devotion to the Blessed Virgin, you will be of the number of her real children, and she will be your mother, under whose protection you shall never perish. Remember well that excellent sentence of St. Anselm, who feared not to say, "That as he must unavoidably perish who has no affection to the Blessed Virgin Mary, and who forsakes her, so it is impossible he should perish who has recourse to her, and whom she regards with an eye of mercy."

I shall conclude with an excellent example which I shall produce for a proof of this truth. St. Bridget had a son who followed the profession of a soldier, and died in the wars. Hearing the news of his death, she was much concerned for the salvation of her son, dead in so dangerous a condition ; and as she was often favoured by God with revelations, of which she has composed a book, she was assured of the salvation of her son by two subsequent revelations. In the first place, the Blessed Virgin revealed to her that she had assisted her son with a particular protection at the hour of death, having strengthened him against temptation, and obtained all necessary grace for him to make a holy and a happy end. In the following, she declared the cause of that singular assistance she gave her son, and said it was the recompense of the great and sincere devotion he had testified to her during his life : wherein he had loved her with a very ardent affection, and had endeavoured to please her in all things.

This, Theotime, is what real devotion to the Blessed Virgin did merit for this young man, and for many others. She will be as powerful in your behalf, if you have a devotion to her, if you love and honour the Blessed Virgin in the manner we have mentioned.

CHAPTER XIII.

Of devotion to our Angel Guardian, and to the Saint of one's name:

God loves us with such tenderness, that he gives to

every one of us an angel for our guardian, employing by His incomparable goodness His most perfect creatures in our service, even those celestial spirits which are created incessantly to contemplate Him and continually to serve him in Heaven. O Theotime, how great is the bounty of God, to depute no less than a prince of his court, for the conduct of a poor servant! and as St. Bernard says, excellently well, "Not to be content to send his Son to us, to give us his holy Spirit, to promise the enjoyment of Himself in Heaven; but to the end there should be nothing in Heaven unemployed for our salvation. He sends his angels to contribute thereto their service; He appoints them our guardians, He commands them to be our masters, and guides.

Entertain particular love and honour for him to whom God has instructed you. He is always near to conduct and guard you: he inspires you with good thoughts; he assists you in important affairs; he fortifies you in temptations; he diverts many misfortunes which otherwise would befall you, whether temporal or spiritual. He continues these good offices in proportion as you have recourse to him.— What is it that you owe not to such a director and guardian?

St. Bernard says, "That the being guarded by our good angel ought to inspire us with three things: respect, love, and confidence. Respect for his presence, love, or devotion for the good will he has for us, and confidence for the care he has of our preservation.

1. Shew, then, Theotime, a great respect to your angel, and when you are tempted to do any wicked action call to mind his presence, and be ashamed to do that before him, which you would not dare to commit before a virtuous person. 2. Love him tenderly, and recommend yourself to him daily. Beseech him that he would direct your actions, and protect you from the misfortunes of this life, and above all from sin, which is the greatest of all evils. 3. Remember to have recourse to him in all your necessities and principally on two occasions.

The first is, when you meditate or undertake any important affair, wherein you have need of counsel and assistance. Entreat your good angel to conduct you in that affair, so that you undertake it not except it be according to the will of God, for his service and your salvation, and to assist in bringing it to a happy issue. This means is very efficacious to make your affairs succeed. It is impossible they should not prosper under so good a guide, who is most faithful, wise, and powerful.

The second is, when you are assaulted with any temptation, and in danger of offending God, " as sften as any tribulation or violent temptation assails you, [says St. Bernard,] implore your guardian, your teacher, your assistant in tribulation." This remedy, Theotime, is very powerful in all temptations, especially in those against chastity, of which the angels are lovers and particular protectors, as being a virtue which makes men like to themselves, and which makes them imitate upon earth their most pure and celestial life. " From whence [says St. Ambrose] it is no wonder if angels defend chaste souls, who lead upon earth a life of angels."

Next to your good angel honour particularly your patron.

The names of Saints are given us at baptism, that they may be our protectors and intercessors with God, and that by their prayers, and the examples of their virtues, we may acquit ourselves worthily of the obligations of a Christian life, whereof we make profession in baptism. " Honour and love him whose name you bear. Recommend yourself daily to him. But to obtain his assistance remember to imitate his virtues."

CHAPTER XlV.

Of Morning Prayer.

Morning and evening prayer, the good employment of time, the knowledge of one's self, reading good books, and pious conversation, are means so necessary to virtue, that respiration and nourishment are not more needful for the support of the corporal life, than these things are necessary for the preservation of piety which is the life of the soul.

I begin with morning prayer, which the wise man, amongst the means he assigns for obtaining wisdom, recommends earnestly to you. "He will give his heart to resort early to the Lord that made him, and he will pray in the sight of the Most High. He will open his mouth in prayer and will make supplication for his sins."

I wish this excellent precept were deeply engraven in the minds of men, and principally of young persons, as one of the most important for living virtuously. If you sincerely aspire to virtue, dear Theotime, you will punctually follow this instruction, which is one of the most necessary you can receive.

We owe to God all our actions, but chiefly the first in the morning; it is that which is most agreeable to him; it is by that we consecrate the rest to him; by it we draw down the Divine blessing upon all our works, and collect the Divine grace for the whole day: as the Israelites in the desert gathered in the morning the manna, which supported them all day.

What is very remarkable in that manna, is, that those who failed to gather it in the morning, found it not presently after, because it was melted at the rising of the sun; whereof the Scripture gives this excellent reason, viz: that God, who showered it down every morning, caused it to be dissolved with the first beams of the sun, "that it might be known to all that we must prevent the sun to bless thee and to adore thee at the dawning of the light."

But remember, Theotime, to perform this action in the manner the wise man prescribes; for he would not have it a constrained, negligent, undevout prayer, but a prayer with the quite contrary qualities; he says, The wise man will give his heart (that is, will apply his will and affection) to resort early to the Lord that made him; that is to say, will give his first thoughts to God, to adore Him as his Creator, and thank him for all his benefits, and he will pray in the sight of the Most High; that is, will consider the greatness of God, who is present, and to whom he speaks, and considering the infinite grandeur of the Divine Majesty, will attentively offer his prayers to him with humility and great modesty, and with a profound respect, begging of God pardon for his sins, and ardently sighing after his holy grace.

To put in execution these instructions, practise what follows. Every morning as soon as you are up cast yourself upon your knees in some retired place, and there,

1. Adore God from your heart, acknowledging Him for your sovereign Master, and Creator, and looking upon him as one from whom you receive all that you have or are.

2. Give him thanks for all the benefits you have received from him; for the favour of your creation, for your redemption by the merits of His Son Jesus-Christ, for making you a Christian, a child of the Catholic church, for instructing you in the necessary truths of salvation and for other particular blesings.

3. Humbly implore his pardon for all the sins of your past life, by which you have so much offended his bounty, and abused his favours.

4. Beg of him the grace to employ that day in his service without offending him : make a firm resolution not to consent to a mortal sin ; purpose to avoid the occasions, and endeavour to forsee those which may happen that day to the end that you may be armed against them

5. Offer all the actions of the day to him, beseeching him that he would bless them, inspire you, and direct you in all your works, that you do nothing against his commandments ; nothing but through him, that is, by His grace ; and nothing but for him, that is, for His glory.

6. Recommend yourself to the Blessed Virgin, to your good angel, and to your patron. Perform all this in a small time, but with much fervour; and be assured, Theotime, that if you be diligent in this exercise, you will find the truth of that saying of wisdom

itself, " They, that in the morning early watch for me shall find me."

Chapter XV.

Of Evening Prayer.

If it be a business of importance to begin the day well, it is of no less to finish it in the same manner. In the old law, God had not only commanded a sacrifice for every morning, but also for every evening: to teach us that we ought to adore Him in the beginning of the day, so we owe Him our acknowledgment at the end of it.

The principal part of this action is the examine of conscience, which is a thing wherein you ought not to fail, if you seriously desire to advance in virtue. 1. It is a powerful means to cure ill habits, to avoid relapsing into sin, or readily to clear one's self of them. 2. It helps to discover the faults one has committed, in order to amend and avoid them, to continue a hatred of mortal sin, and a will not to commit it any more. 3. Without the exercise, we fall into many offences, which, being neglected, leads us into mortal sin (we are lulled asleep when in sin,) without a desire or thought of freeing ourselves. . 4. By this exercise, ordinary confessions are made more easy and frequent; we amend our lives; we prevent an unprovided death; we prepare ourselves for judgment by judging ourselves. And it is in this condition that we excellently practice that admirable advice of the wise man : " Before judgment, examine thyself, and thou shalt find mercy in the sight of God."

Be careful, then, Theotime, to perform daily this important exercise in the following manner. At night, being upon your knees, before you go to bed,—1. Adore God and give Him thanks for all his favours, particularly for preserving you that day from misfortunes, which might have befallen you.

2. Beg of Him grace to discover the sins you have committed that day, in order to ask pardon for them and amend your life.

3. Examine your conscience concerning the sins to which you are most subject. For this effect, call

to mind your chief actions from morning to night, and take·notice of the faults you have 'committed. Recollect whether you have had any temptations that day, examine how you behaved, whether you have readily resisted them, or with negligence. Take notice what company you have been in, and whether you have done anything indecently, either by giving ill example in word or deed, either in yourself or others; for example either through persuasion, fear of displeasing or being despised, or in a word by not preventing the sin of another when in your power. Consider whether you have well employed your time all that day, or unprofitably lost it; and so of the rest.

4. After discovering the sins you have committed, stir up in yourself a sorrow for them, humbly beg pardon of God, make a resolution to amend the day following, and remember to confess them the first opportunity.

If unhappily amongst these sins there should be any that are mortal, rise not up from your prayers till you have amply deplored your 'misery, and conceived an extreme regret for having so grievously offended so holy and adorable a God. Beg of Him pardon with all the contrition of your heart, and protest that you will confess it as soon as possible. Beg of Him that you may not die in that wretched state. Alas! dear Theotime, is it possible a soul can sleep without fear, and dread, whilst under the weight of mortal sin? If you have no such dread, you ought to look upon such an insensibility with horror, as a snare by which the Devil endeavours to ruin you for ever.

5. Recommend to God your soul and body, beg of Him that he will preserve you from all misfortune that night, and principally from sin. Offer your prayers to the Blessed Virgin, your angel guardian, your patron, and the saints together. ·And, as in the beginning of the day, you begged of God the grace to live well, so at the end remember to beg of Him the grace to die well. The end we make of every day, is emblematical of the end we shall one day make of our lives. Finish therefore, every day, as you would one day, finish your life.

F

CHAPTER XVI.

Of the fear of God.

The first virtue that is necessary for you, Theotime, is the fear of God; it is that which, next to faith, is the basis and groundwork of all others. The Scripture calls it "the beginning of wisdom;" and it teacheth us that it is the first thing that ought to be inspired into young souls. For this reason, Solomon, instructing youth in his Proverbs, begins his instruction with this excellent precept, so often repeated in Scripture, "The fear of the Lord is the beginning of wisdom." And the same Scripture, in the history of the Holy Tobias, observes expressly, that having a child, from his infancy he taught him to fear God, and to abstain from all sin.

By this fear, we must not understand a gross and servile fear, that stands in awe of nothing but the punishment which it apprehends, more than the offence; but a respectful fear, by which, considering the greatness and Majesty of his sanctity, God, his power, his justice, we conceive a profound respect, and apprehend above all things to fall, by mortal sin, into the displeasure of a God so great, so holy, so powerful, so just.

This, Theotime, is the fear of God, which is the beginning of wisdom and the foundation of true piety. It is this to which I exhort you here, and which you chiefly should aim to acquire. 1. Beg it daily of God, who is the author of it; say to him frequently from the bottom of your heart, "Pierce thou my flesh with thy fear, for I am afraid of Thy judgments." 2. Conceive an awful respect for the Majesty of God. He is the Sovereign Lord of all things, infinite in His perfections, in majesty, in wisdom in goodness, in power, in justice. All creatures adore him; the angels themselves tremble at the sight of His immensity. All that is great in the world, is but an atom in his sight; and as he has created all things by one word, so He could destroy them all in a moment. There is none like to thee. O Lord: Thou art great, and great is thy name in might, who shall not fear

Thee, O King of Nations! Fear above all things to displease God; and let that be the first and principal thing you regard in all your actions, whether God be not therein offended. 3. When you speak of God, never speak of him but with profound respect; and endeavour to cause by your example, that He never be spoken of otherwise in your presence.

CHAPTER XVII.

Of the Love of God.

If the greatness of God obliges us to fear and honour Him with profound respect, His goodness engages us as much to love Him. We must fear God by reason of his greatness, which renders him infinitely adorable; and we must love Him because of his goodness, which makes him infinitely amiable. We must not separate these two virtues, fear and love. The fear of God is the beginning of his love, and love is the perfection of fear. He that is without fear, cannot be justified. He that is, loveth not; abideth in death.

We must then love God, dear Theotime, for how can it be that you should not love goodness itself, and Him who hath loved you first? But you must love him betimes, and from your tender years: you must begin that early, which you must do all your life, and during all eternity. The love of our God is our last end. God has placed you in this world for no other end than to love Him; and that coming to know Him for your Creator, you should render that which a work owes to its workmen, a creature to its Creator, a child to its father, that is love. And to induce you the better, thereunto, He has added all imaginable favours. having designed you for the enjoyment of his kingdom in Heaven, redeemed you when you were lost, and redeemed you by the death of his only Son, called you to the grace of Christianity, enlightened you with faith, sanctified you by his grace, received you often into his mercy, and replaced you among his children, after you had grievously offended him; and a thousand other blessings has He bestowed upon you. Theotime, how is it possible not to love God, who has loved you so much?

There are two things in God for which He ought to be beloved. The one is his goodness, which He manifests unto us by all the favours and blessings which He bestows upon us. The other is the goodness He possesses in himself, which makes him transcendantly amiable. For, if we might suppose a thing impossible, viz., that God had never showed us any favour, yet He deserves to be infinitely beloved, by reason of the sovereign goodness and infinite perfections He enjoys in himself, which render Him infinitely amiable. When I say we must love God, I conclude a twofold love: the first is, for the benefits He has bestowed upon us; the second in consideration of his infinite goodness, which renders him so lovely, that in the love of his goodness consists the eternal happiness of both men and angels.

But take notice Theotime, that the love of God, to be real, ought to have one very particular condition which occurs not in any other love; for it does not suffice to love God as we love creatures, but we must love Him above all things, that is, more than all creatures. Thou shalt love the Lord thy God with thy whole heart; that is, more than all other things; so that you love nothing .above Him, as there is nothing greater or more amiable than he; not anything equal to Him, as there is nothing which can equal Him.

In a word, the love of God consists in preferring God above all things, before the goods of the world, pleasures, honours, and life itself; so that you must be prepared never to love these things to the prejudice of the love you owe to God; and be resolved rather to lose them a thousand times than be wanting in the obedience you are obliged to render unto Him. It is in this preference of God above all things the essential point of the love of God consist; a preference, without which it is impossible to love God, or to be in the state of salvation.

You must then labour early to acquire this so amiable love, and this so necessary a preference, to engrave it deep in your heart; and to the end you be not deceived therein, by taking as very many do, apparent love for the real, see the principal acts you must practice therein by which you may know whether you love God truly or not. 1. Above all things, fear and have a horror of sin because it is displeasing to God, and infinitely opposite to his goodness, and he resolved never to commit a sin upon any account whatsoever. 2. Fly venial sins as much as possible, because they displease God; and although they destroy not His love, yet they diminish and weaken it, and dispose you to fall into mortal sin. 3. Labour to acquire the virtues so necessary for you, and which He requires of you. It is the property of love, to desire to please him whom one loves. If you love God, dear Theotime, you will be careful not only to preserve your-self in his holy grace, by avoiding sin, but you will en-deavour to acquire those virtues you know will make you most acceptable to Him. 4. Often in your heart and with your lips, form acts of the love of God; wish often that God be served and loved as he deserves. Be troubled when you see him offended; hinder it as much as you can; and endeavour by your words and example to move others to love him. 5. Begin from youth to love Him whom you must never cease to love. At what time soever you begin to love Him, it will be always too late, and you will always have reason to express that grief which St. Augustin did: "I have loved Thee too late, O ancient Beauty! I have loved Thee too late, O eternal Goodness!" Beg of Him fervently the grace to love him as you ought, and daily say to Him from your heart, those excellent words of David: O God, what have I in Heaven? and, besides Thee, what do I desire upon earth? Thou art the God of my heart, and the God that is my portion for ever.

CHAPTER XVIII.

Of the love of Parents.

He that feareth the Lord, says the wise man, honor-eth his parents, and will serve them as his masters

that brought him into the world. Yes, Theotime, if
you have the fear of God in your heart, you will honour your parents, and all those to whom He has given
authority over you, because it is His will and command.
Honour thy father and thy mother; and if you honour them not, you have neither the fear nor the love of
God.

For to contemn a duty, which nature herself dictates,
and which God has so strictly commanded, is not to have
the fear of God. There is no menace which He has not
denounced against those children who are wanting in this
duty. He saith, he that afflicteth his father, and chaseth
away his mother, is infamous and unhappy. He that curseth
his father and mother, his lamp shall be put out in the
midst of darkness. The eye that mocketh at his father,
and that despiseth the labour of his mother in bearing him,
let the ravens of the brooks pick it out, and the young
eagles eat it. Of what evil fame is he that forsaketh his
father! and he is cursed of God that angereth his mother.
I wish these menaces were deeply engraved on the minds of
all children, who forget ever so little their duty towards
their parents.

Render then to your parents, Theotime, the honour you
owe them, considering: 1. That it is just and reasonable.
2. That God will have it so; God, I say, whose will ought
to be the rule of our actions, and whose command is the
most powerful motive to a generous soul. The honour you
ought to give to your parents, includes four principal things,
which you owe to them, viz., respect, love, obedience, and
assistance.

1. Bear them great respect, considering them as those
from whom, next to God, you have received your being.
Never despise them upon any consideration whatever:
either interiorly, by any thought of contempt, or exteriorly
by any words or disrespectful behaviour. Receive with
good will their instructions, admonitions, and reprimands.
My son, says the wise man, hear the instruction of thy
father, and forsake not the law of thy mother. A fool
laugheth at the instruction of his father; but he that re-
gardeth reproofs, shall become prudent.

2. Entertain an affectionate love for them. Remember, says the wise man, that thou hadst not been born but through them; and make a return to them. Now this can only be done by loving them. Yet, take notice, that this love must not only be a natural and sensible love: it must also be a rational love, and according to God. To love them according to God, you must love them because God commands it ; and as he commands it, that is in such a manner that you love principally their spiritual good and salvation: and endeavour to procure it by your prayers, and all other means which lie in your power.

3. Shew a ready obedience to them, as holding the place of God: yet only, as St. Paul advises, in the Lord, because such is his will ; for it is God who commands you to obey them; and when you obey them, you obey God, as, on the contrary, not obeying them, you disobey God, except they command any thing against the honour of God, or your good; for in those two cases, you owe them no obedience. Nevertheless you must be very discreet on such an occasion, and procure the best advice, that you may not be deceived.

4. You must assist them in their necessities, in sickness, poverty, old age, and generally in all their temporal and spiritual necessities. To forsake them on such occasion, is a very great crime, which cries to God for vengeance.

CHAPTER XIX.

Of other Persons whom Youth ought to Honour.

Next to your parents, there are other persons you ought particularly to honour.

1. You must honour those who represent them, your tutors, and those who have a charge of your person ; your elder brothers and sisters, for to them there is a respect due.

2. Your masters, whether private or public, from whom you receive instruction in virtue and learning.— You ought to honour them by so much more, as they

represent your parents, and as the benefits you receive from them, such as virtue and knowledge, (the ornaments of the mind,) far surpass all wordly riches.   And as you owe to your parents respect, love, obedience, and assistance; you also owe to your masters, respect, love, obedience, and gratitude.

3. You owe a special honour to your spiritual masters, such as your pastors, and all those who instruct you in the way of salvation, and chiefly your ghostly father.— Respect him much, regarding him as an officer of God; love him as the minister of your salvation; obey him, and follow his advice, in which young people are often very defective.

4. Honour all the persons that are venerable: either for dignity as priests, whom the Scripture commands you to honour; or for their age, as old men, to whom young people should shew much respect; or for their virtue (for if you honour God, you will also honour them that serve him); and lastly, men in public authority, whom God commands you to honour, as representing his place, and whom He has established for his ministers in the temporal government of mankind.

CHAPTER XX.

Of Swearing and Lying.

To be addicted to swearing is a very vicious quality, especially in young people. I speak not of oaths appointed by religion to ascertain a truth, when sufficient necessity requires it, a necessity which seldom happens to young people; but of those oaths so common among Christians, where the adorable name of God is called upon and taken in vain, in the least anger or impatience, and sometimes of swearing deliberately, from a detestable custom, by the name of God on all occasions.

This sin is one of the most fatal habits a man can contract: For, 1st. It is a contempt of God, to respect so little his holy name, which all creatures adore, and whose sanctity makes all the angels to tremble; and this notwithstanding God's express prohibition.—

"Thou shalt not take the name of the Lord thy God in vain." 2. It is an heinous outrage offered to his Son Jesus Christ, to treat with so much irreverence, the precious death he suffered for our redemption, and the adorable blood he shed for our salvation; an outrage which is no less than that he received by the cruelty of his executioners. "He was scourged [says St. Augustin] with the rods of the Jews, and he is now scourged by the blasphemous tongues of wicked Christians. And they sin no less, who blaspheme Jesus Christ reigning in Heaven, than those who blasphemed him when he walked upon Earth." 3. This vice causes many other sins to be committed, for besides that there is no sin multiplies like swearing, when grown habitual, it draws the curse of God upon those who are accustomed to it, by which they are abandoned to their passions, and to the occasions of sin; for this reason the wise man said, "A man that sweareth much shall be filled with iniquity and a scourge shall not depart from his house." 4. This vice is very hard to be corrected; though ever so little rooted, it increases still with age, and becomes at length past remedy, as those who are subject to it, do daily experience. Lastly, it suffices to say, that this sin is the sin of the devils, who are pleased in nothing but in abusing the holy name of God. And it is a horrible thing that Christians, who ought to praise God upon Earth, as the angels praise him in Heaven, should offer him here the same injuries as the devils throw out against him in hell.

O Theotime, fly this detestable sin, abominable before God and man, odious in persons of every age, but principally in youth. Remember that the ancient law condemned blasphemers to death, and St. Paul delivered over to the Devil two Christians guilty of this crime; that they may learn, says he, not to blaspheme. And St. Gregory relates, how a child accustomed to swear, in his impatience, by the name of God, was seized with a mortal distemper and assaulted by evil spirits, which caused him to depart this life in his father's arms, who being too indulgent in cor-

recting him, had bred up, in this child, a great sinner for
Hell, as the same Saint observes:

The remedy of this sin, when one has ever so little
a habit or inclination to it, is to fly the causes, as anger,
gaming wicked company, and all other things which every
one knows to be, of themselves, an occasion of swearing.
But above all it is a powerful, and even necessary remedy,
to impose upon one's self some rigorous punishment every
time he shall fall into this sin ; as some alm, some prayers
to be performed the same day, some fasting to be observed
soon after, or other mortifications.

Avoid every degree of oath or imprecations, and other
phrases, which though not oaths, tend to swearing upon occasions. Christian modesty requires that we should not
swear at all : according to that holy precept of our Saviour
" I say to you not to swear at all, but let your speech be
Yea, yea ; for whatsoever is more than these cometh of
evil."

Beware also of lying Theotime, which is not the least
considerable among the sins of the tongue ; and it is so much
more important that you should be solidly instructed on this
subject, as it is frequent with young persons, and infinitely
pernicious when once become habitual. A lie is always
a sin, because it is always against truth, known to be such
by him who speaks : and although it be not a mortal sin, when
it is not a matter of consequence, nevertheless, the habit
of lying although lightly, is not a light thing, nor of small
importance.

A habit or custom of lying opens a gate to an infinite
number of other vices. A lying person will become a cheat
and deceiver in his behaviour, double in his words, unfaith-
ful in his promises, a hypocrite in his manners, a dissembler
in his actions, a flatterer and faint-hearted when he should
speak truth ; bold and shameless to affirm lies, impudent to
maintain them as certain truths, a swearer, detractor, mis-
trustful of every one ; for as he is accustomed to lie, he
believes that others always speak false. A mind addicted
to lying, will easily be so in things of moment, and conse-
quently in heinous sins.   .

So that, Theotime, there are few vices more pernicious, and principally to youth, than this custom of
lying. For this reason, be not willing to make any
manner of lie for the custom thereof is not good ; that
is, according to the expression of the Scripture, it is very
bad.

In a word, it is so wicked a quality of the mind to be
a liar, that the Scripture speaks of it in unusual terms. It
says that God abhors it: that lying lips are an abomi-
nation to the Lord ; as, on the contrary, those who love
sincerity in their words, gain his friendship. Thou, O
Lord, wilt destroy all that speak a lie. Lying is infamous
among men. A lie is a foul blot in a man, and yet it will
be continually in the mouth of men without discipline. A
thief is better than a man that is always lying ; but both of
them shall inherit destruction.

Lastly, this vice makes men resemble the Devil, who is
pleased with nothing more than lies. It was he who in-
vented it, and who is the father thereof, as the Son of God
has named him with his own mouth.

St. Augustin says, "That as the truth comes from
God, lying takes it origin from the Devil." And St.
Ambrose adds, " That those who love lying, are the children of that detestable fiend, for the children of God love
truth."

Fly entirely, Theotime, this pernicious vice in all occur-
rences, but chiefly in two.

1. When you speak of a thing of importance, that is
when it prejudices your neighbour in his goods, honour, or
eternal welfare, wherein you must be very cautions, and
even more than in regard of yourself.

2. When you speak to a person who has authority,
over you : for then a lie is a very culpable imposture, as
well by reason of the respect you then break through,
as because it frequently happens that those falsehoods
notably prejudice your own good ; or that of your neighbour, which you are obliged to promote when it is in your
power.

Lastly, in whatsoever matter it be, and to whatsoever person you speak, accustom yourself never to tell

a lie on purpose or with reflection. Love truth and sincerity
in all your words. What an excellent quality it is in a young
man, when he cannot tell an untruth without blushing! The
just, says the wise man, shall hate a lying word. Beg of God
that he give you a hatred of this sin, and frequently offer him
that prayer of Solomon, Remove far from me vanity and lying
words.

CHAPTER XXI.

Of Sports and Recreations.

Recreation is necessary to relax the spirits, particularly of young
people; and that which is taken in innocent diversion is most
proper for them, it being more proportioned to their nature, and
the capacity of their mind.

Pastime, then, and recreation are not contrary to virtue, but
rather commanded; and it is an act of virtue when it is done as it
ought.

To be such, it is necessary above all things that the motive be good; that is, that it be taken to recreate the mind,
and to make it more capable of labour, which it could not be
able to undergo, if it were always employed. So that labour
is the end, and motive of sport and recreation. We recreate
ourselves on account of the fatigue we have undergone, and
in order to undergo more. From hence three conditions follow,
which must be observed in pastime, that it may be good and
virtuous.

The first, to observe moderation; for excess herein renders
it no longer a recreation, but rather an employment; for it would
not then be taken to prepare us for new labour, which is the sole
end pastime ought to have, but merely for our pleasure, which is
a vicious end; yea, it is to make one unfit for labour, because
excess in amusement dissipates the spirits, enfeebles the powers of
the body, and often times considerably prejudices the health, by
the distempers it causes.

The second condition is, not to have an irregular affection
for amusements, as it happens frequently to young persons. This
affection makes them fall into the excess just mentioned, lose
much time, and think continually on the means of dissipation.
It generally prevents their applying themselves seriously to labour, and when their body is at study, their mind is bent upon
their sport and divertisement.

The third condition is, to fly as much as possible from
games of hazard, which enslaves the minds principally of youths
and instead of refreshing the spirits, load them with anxiety;
one is there so deeply concerned in losing or winning that it
is hard to observe moderation. They play there only out of
covetousness and for gain, which is a criminal motive; con-

sider also the ordinary losses one suffers, which leave after them displeasure, vexation, and despair; add to these cheats, unjust gain, cholor, swearing, quarrels, with which these sorts of games are ordinarily attended; the great loss of time, the dissipation of mind and goods, the sinful habits of anger, of impatience, of swearing, of lying, of covetousness, a neglect of duty to God and their family, and adherence to ill company, an aversion to what is serious, and a love to be idle, and to make their life but a change or succession of idleness. Such an unhappy inclination to play frequently continues all their life, to the ruin of their wealth and honour, and reduces them to the utmost misery, as we daily see by too many examples, and in short makes a man incapable of all good.

Avoid all prohibited games, Theotime, as absolutely inconsistent with your salvation; amuse yourself in some laudable diversion, which may serve to unbend the mind, or exercise the body, observing therein the conditions we have spoken of, especially avoiding all excess, which St. Augustin, in his confessions, acknowledged to be one of the causes of the wickedness of his youth. Now this excess is understood, not only of the time employed therein, which ought always to be very little; otherwise you will play for gain, and not for recreation, and the sport will be a rack and disquiet rather than a diversion. Besides, the money you lose at play would be better employed amongst the poor, whose necessity will cry one day to God against your excesces, and those of all gamesters.

CHAPTER XXII.

The conclusion of all that has been said in the foregoing Chapters.

It is certainly, Theotime, of great consequence that you should be virtuous in your younger years, and that the good or evil life of youth is not trifling, nor a thing that deserves little care or regard, as the greatest part of the world thinks; but that it is a business of high importance, the truth of which is founded upon all that is great and sacred, in what concerns the service of God, and salvation of men.

1. You are obliged to serve God in your youth, because you ought to acknowledge Him as your Creator and sovereign Master, for the being you have received from Him, and on account of the most sublime and excellent end for which He has created you; having made you for nothing less than to possess Him eternally in heaven, after you have faithfully served Him upon earth.

2. On account of the great favour he has shown you in calling you to Christianity and the Catholic religion, out of

which all those who obstinately remain cannot be saved.

3. Because the service of young people is singularly pleasing to God, since He loves them with a particular affection, and is pleased to confer many benefits upon them.

4. Because you cannot refuse Him your service, without offering Him a heinous injury.

5. Because He hath an incredible aversion to wicked young people.

6. Because your eternal salvation has a great dependence upon the life you lead in your youth; so that if you set your affection upon virtue in your younger years, you will easily preserve it the remainder of your life : and if you follow vice, you cannot withdraw yourself but with great difficulty, and perhaps not at all.

1. To avoid the heavy misfortunes which spring from the wicked life of youth, untimely death, obdurateness in sin, the loss of many fair hopes, and the overflowing of vice amongst men.

8. And, lastly, because of the persecution which the devil raises against young people, whom he continually endeavours to withdraw from the services of God, and ensnares betimes in disorders, that he may destroy them without recovery.

After all these reasons, I ask you, whether you, now hesitate what you have to do? Are not these considerations powerful enough to convince you of the obligation you have to consecrate yourself to virtue in your youth? And if you be convinced thereof, what do you mean? What is your design and resolution for the future? Perhaps hitherto you have not comprehended the greatness of obligation ; but now, understanding it clearly, what judgment ought you not to expect from God, if you be rebellious to the light, and act like those wretches who say to God, Depart from us, we desire not the knowledge of thy ways.

The Jews being returned from the captivity of Babylon, the prophet Esdras caused the law of God to be publicly read unto them, from whence they had received no instruction during the seventy years of their captivity.

That people had scarce begun to hear the law, when they wept bitterly, and made the air resound with their cries and lamentations : so that the priests and Levites who read the law, were more employed to stop their tears, and comfort, than instruct them. This poor people sadly deplored their unhappy ignorance of their duty ; an ignorance which their own negligence had occasioned.

O, dear Theotime, I beseech the Divine Goodness by His grace to work the same effect in your heart. After reading the truths

I have represented to you, is it possible that you should not be touched with the force of truth and the care of your salvation? And that after reading all these reasons which show the strict obligation you have to the service of your Creator, you should shut the book without making any reflections upon yourself, or taking proper resolutions for the future? I conjure you by the honour and respect you owe to God, by the love you owe to His Son Jesus Christ, your gracious Saviour; by the concern you ought to have for your eternal salvation; I conjure you, I say, that you do not read these truths unprofitable; and that when you have read them, you do not cast the book out of your hands, until you have made a full resolution to think seriously on your salvation; to that effect, firmly resolve to lead a virtuous life during your youth, preserveing the grace you have received; or correcting your past life by a holy and virtuous one, if it has been disorderly.

It is here, where you must open your eyes to see yourself, and deplore your past offences, and the blindness which has produced them, saying with St. Augustin, "Wo, wo be to the darkness wherein I have lived! wo to the blindness, which hath hindered me from seeing the light of heaven! wo to my past ignorance, wherein I knew not thee! I give thee thanks, O God, whom I acknowledge to be my illuminator and redeemer, because thou hast enlightened me with thy grace, so that now I know thee. I have known thee too late. O ancient *Truth!* I have known thee late. O eternal *Verity!*'

PART III.

THE PRINCIPAL FESTIVALS EXPOUNDED.

SUNDAY was dedicated by the Apostles to the more particular service and honour of Almighty God, and transferred from Saturday, the Jewish Sabbath, which they then abolished, to the day following, in memory that Christ our Lord rose from the dead, and sent down the Holy Ghost on that day, whence it is called the Lord's day : and, Sunday, from the heathens dedicating it to the Sun.

The four Sundays of Advent, preceding, Christmas, were instituted by the Church with particular offices, commemorative of the benefits of our Saviour's coming to redeem the world by his happy birth.

The four *Ember weeks,* in Latin *Quatuor tempora,* are times of public prayer, fasting, and procession, partly instituted for the successful ordination of priests and ministers of the church, and partly to beg and give thanks to God for the fruits of the earth. *Ember* is derived from the Greek word *emera*, a day ; others call them *Ember days*, from the ancient religious custom of eating nothing on those days till night, and then only a cake baked under the embers, called ember-bread.

Septuagesima, *Sexagesima*, and *Quinquagesima Sundays*, are days set apart for acts of penance and mortification, and a certain graduation or preparation to the devotion of Lent; being more proper and immediate to the passion and resurrection of Christ ; taking their numeral denomination from their being about seventy, sixty, and fifty days before Easter.

Shrovetide signifies the time of confession ; for our Saxon ancestors used to say, " We will go to shrift ;" and, in the more primitive times, it was the custom of all good Christians then to confess their sins to a priest, the better to prepare themselves for a holy observance of Lent, and worthily receiving the blessed sacrament at Easter.

Ash Wednesday is a day of public penance and humiliation in the whole Church of God, so called from the ceremony of blessing ashes, wherewith the priest signs the people with a cross on their forehead, giving them this wholesome admonition ' Remember, man, thou art dust, and unto dust thou shalt return,' Gen. iii. 9, to remind them of their mortality, and prepare them for the holy fast of Lent. The ashes are made of the palms blessed on the Palm Sunday of the preceding year.

Lent, an old Saxon word signifying Spring ; this fast being observed in the beginning of the year, and in Latin is called *Quadragesima*, because it is a fast of forty days, except Sundays, which are only abstinence, instituted by the church. Many are the motives for which Lent is established. 1. This fast is the figure of the spirit of Penance, which every one of the faithful ought to conserve throughout the whole of his life. 2. It is, as it were a tithe or tenth, which the faithful offer to God, sanctifying by fasting these forty days, which make about a tenth part of the year. 3. This fast is a weak Imitation of what Jesus-Christ our Lord performed in the desert, in fasting forty days and forty nights, without eating or drinking. 4. It was appointed in consequence of the obligation which Christ our Lord imposed on his disciples, t o fast after his ascension. 5. By this fast we participate in the sufferings of our Lord, in order to have a share in his glory. And, lastly, it prepares us to celebrate worthily, the approaching Easter.

Passion Sunday, so called from the passion of Christ then

drawing nigh, was ordained by the Church more closely to prepare us for a worthy celebration of that solemnity.   On this day the crucifixes, &c., in churches, are covered with a mourning colour ; both to commemorate our Saviour's going out of the temple and hiding himself, and to dispose us to compassionate his sufferings.

Palm-Sunday, in memory and honour of our Lord's triumphant entry into Jerusalem, is so called from the palm branches strewed under his feet by the Hebrew children, crying, Hosanna to the son of David. Matt. xxi. And therefore the church this day blesses palms, and makes a solemn procession, in memory of that humble triumph of our Saviour, the people bearing palm branches in their hands.

Maunday Thursday, in memory, of our Lord's last supper, when he instituted the blessed sacrament of his body and blood, is so called from the first of the anthem *Mandatum,* &c., John xviii. 34, I gave you a new command, that you love one another as I have loved you ; which is sung on that day in the choir, when the prelate begins the ceremony of washing the people's feet in imitation of Christ's washing those of his disciples, before He instituted the blessed sacrament.

Good Friday is the anniversary of that most sacred and memorable day on which the great work of our redemption was consummated, by our Saviour Jesus Christ, on his bloody cross, between two thieves, on Mount Calvary, near Jerusalem.

On, Thursday, Friday and Saturday, in Holy Week, the offices called *Tenebre,* were formerly mournfully sung in lamentation of our Lord's passion. But because the offices are now anticipated on the evening of Wednesday, Thursday, and Friday, they have obtained the names of 'Tenebræ days, for that *Tenebræ,* or darkness, which overspread the face of the earth, at the time of his passion ; for which end all the lights are extinguished : and after some silence at the end of the offices, a noise is made to represent the rending of the veil of the temple, and the disorder in which all nature was involved at the death of our divine Redeemer.

Easter-Day, in Latin, *pascha,* a great festival in memory and honour of our Saviour's resurrection from the dead, on the third day after his crucifixion, Matt. xxviii. 6. It is called Easter from Oriens, the east or raising, one of Christ's titles. And his name, says the prophet Zacharias, chap. vi. 12, is Oriens. 'This is the day our Lord has made, let us rejoice and be glad in it.' The church repeating frequently these words on this day, desires that her children, after having shared in the sufferings of Christ, by compunction and penance, should participate in the glory and joy of his resurrection by a lively faith, hoping to rise again themselves, by an ardent love, with their Redeemer, who having died in satisfaction for our sins, is risen again for our justification; and, finally, by a new life, pure, and wholly celestial. The Monday following is also kept holy, in memory of our Lord's first appearance after his resurrection, which is commemorated on this day, for the greater solemnity of the festival.

Low-Sunday, in Latin *Dominica in albais*, the Octave of Easter-day, is so called from the catechumens' white garments, emblems of innocence and joy, which they put on at their baptism, and solemnly put off this day.

Rogation-Week, the next but one before Whitsunday, is so called from *rogo*, to ask or pray; because on Monday, Tuesday, and Wednesday, the Litanies are sung; and abstinence from flesh is enjoined by the church, not only as a devout preparative to the feast of Christ's glorious Ascension and Pentecost, but also to supplicate the blessing of God on the fruit of the earth. The Belgians call it Cruis, or Cross-Week, and so it is called in some parts of England : because, when the priest goes on those days in procession, the cross is carried before him. In the north of England it is called Gang-Week, from the 'ganging,' or procession then used.

Ascension Day, a feast solemnized in memory of Christ's glorious ascension into heaven, on the fortieth day after his resurrection, in the sight of his apostles and disciples— Acts i. 9.

Whit-Sunday, or *Pentecost*, a solemn feast in memory and honour of the descent of the Holy Ghost on the apostles, in the form of tongues of fire, Acts ii. 3. Pentecost, in Greek, signifies the fiftieth day after his resurrection. It is called Whit-Sunday, from the catechumens being anciently clothed in white, and admitted, on the eve of this feast, to the sacrament of baptism. The old Saxons called it Weed, or Holy-Sunday. In the law of Moses, this day was most solemn. It is believed, that on it God gave the law to Moses upon Mount Sinai. On that day, people offered to God the first fruits of the earth. The faithful ought to beg of God to be filled with the Holy-Ghost, and to participate of the grace, the light, and charity, and strength, which the same Holy-Ghost communicated to the first Christians, the following Monday is also a holiday of obligation, and the faithful ought to apply themselves in this week more than usual to the work of mercy.

Trinity-Sunday, the Octave of Whit-Sunday, is dedicated to the honour of the blessed Trinity ; to signify that the work of our redemption and sanctification, then completed, are common to the Three Divine Persons.

Corpus Christi, the Thursday after Trinity Sunday, is a feast instituted by the church in honor of the Blessed sacrament of the altar; it receives its denomination from the body of Christ, substantially present therein. On this day, in all Catholic countries, that adorable sacrament is solemnly carried in procession, the priest and people expressing their highest devotion in hymns and prayers, accompanied by several other exterior testimonies of pious affection, such as music, flowers strewed along the streets, and their walls covered with the richest tapestries.

JANUARY.

1st.—*The Circumcision of our Lord* is called New Year's Day, from the Romans beginning their year on it. This feast is instituted by the church in memory of our Lord's Circumcision on the eighth day after his nativity, according to the precept of the old law, Gen. xxii. 12. when he was called JESUS, as the angel has foretold, Luke i. 32, and began to shed his infant blood by the stony knife of circumcision.

6th.—*The Epiphany of our Lord* is a feast solemnised in memory and honor of Christ's manifestation to the Gentiles, by an extraordinary star, which conducted the three kings from the east to adore Him in the manger, where they presented Him with gold, myrrh, and frankincense, in token of his divinity, regality, and humanity, or his being God, King and Man. The word *Epiphany* is derived from the Greek, which signifies manifestation. It is also called Twelfth-Day, on account of its being celebrated the twelfth day after Christ's birth, exclusively. On the same day are commemorated our Saviour's baptism, and his first miracle of turning water into wine, at the wedding of Cana, in Galilee.

FEBRUARY.

2d.—The Purification of the Blessed Virgin, or *Candlemas Day*, is a feast in commemoration and honour both of the Presentation of our blessed Lord, and the Purification of our Lady in the Temple of Jerusalem, the fortieth day after her happy delivery, performed according to the law of Moses, Lev. xii. It is called Purification from the Latin *Purifico*, which signifies to purify; not that the Blessed Virgin had contracted anything by her child-birth which needed purifying, being the Mother of Purity itself, but because common mothers were, by this ceremonial rite, freed from the legal impurity of child-birth, to which out of her great humility, she submitted. It is also called Candlemas-Day, because, before Mass on that Day, the church blesses her candles for the whole year, and makes a procession with blessed candles in the hands of the faithful in memory of the light wherewith Christ illuminated the whole church at his presentation, when old Simeon styled him, a "light to lighten the Gentiles, and the glory of his people Israel." Luke ii. 32.

24—St. Matthias, chosen by the College of Apostles, to supply the place of Judas the traitor; he suffered Martyrdom, anno, 74.

MARCH.

17.—St. Patrick, apostle of Ireland. He was a Briton by birth, and nephew to St. Martin, Bishop of Tours. Being sent, in 443, by Pope Celestinus, to convert the Irish to Christianity, he entered upon his ministry with such piety and courage, that he subdued the inhabitants to the laws of the gospel of Christ; and after having governed the church of Ireland sixty years, during which he is said to have consecrated 305 Bishops, and ordained 3,000 Priests, he died in the odour of sanctity, at the age of 123 years.

19.—St. Joseph, the reputed father of our blessed Saviour, and spouse of our blessed Lady.

25.—*Annunciation of our Lady*, a feast in memory of the Angel Gabriel's most happy embassy, when, by her consent and the cooperation of the Holy Ghost, the Son of God was incarnate in her sacred womb.

APRIL.

25.—St. Mark, evangelist, the disciple and interpreter of St. Peter, writing his gospel at the request of the Christians at Rome, he took it with aim into Egypt; first preaching at Alexandria, he founded that Church; and afterwards, being apprehended for the faith of Christ, was bound with cords, dragged upon stones, and shut up in a close prison, where he was comforted by an angelic vision, and apparition of our Lord. Finally, he was called to heaven in the eighth year of Nero. On this day the long litanies are said or sung, and abstinence from flesh is observed, to obtain the blessing of God, on the fruits of the earth.

MAY.

1st.—SS. Philip and James, Apostles. After the first had converted almost all Scythia to the faith of Christ, being fastened to a cross, he was stoned to death, making a glorious end at Hieropolis, in Asia, in the year fifty-four. The second, called also our Lord's brother, was the first bishop of Jerusalem, where, being thrown from a pinnacle of the temple, his thighs broken, and struck on the head with a fuller's club, he gave up the ghost, and was buried near the temple, in the year sixty-three.

3.—*Finding the Holy Cross*, otherwise called, *Holy Blood Day.* A feast in memory of the miraculous discovery of the holy cross whereon our Saviour suffered, by St. Helen, mother of Constantine the Great, in the year three hundred and twenty-six, after it had been concealed by the Infidels one hundred and eight years, who erected a statue of Venus in place of it.

JUNE.

11.—St. Barnaby ; born at Cyprus, and ordained apostle of the Gentiles by St. Paul. He travelled with him into many provinces exercising the function of preaching the gospel committed to him ; and lastly, going into Cyprus, there adorned his apostleship with a glorious crown of martyrdom in the year fifty-six. His body, by a revelation of himself, was found in the times of Zeno the emperor, with St. Matthew's gospel in his own handwriting,

24.—*Nativity of St. John Baptist*, our Lord's precursor, the son of Zachary and Elizabeth, who being yet in the mother's womb, was replenished with the Holy-Ghost.

29.—St. Peter and St. Paul are joined in one solemnity, because they were the principal co-operators under Christ, in the conversion of the world ; the first having converted the Jews, the other the Gentiles. They were both martyred at the same place, Rome, on the same day.

JULY.

2 —*Visitation of our B. Lady*, a feast instituted to commemorate the visit she paid her cousin, St. Elizabeth, immediately after she had received the angel's message of the incarnation of the Son of God. It is celebrated at this time, when it is probable she returned to Nazareth, rather than at the exact time she undertook it, about Easter ; because its observance at that holy season can scarcely be complied with, on account of the many great solemnities then occurring. This feast was instituted by Pope Urbain VI, in the year thirteen hundred and eighty-five.

25.—St. James, called the Great, brother to St. John the Evangelist, was, about the feast of Easter, beheaded at Jerusalem y Herod Agrippa, in the year forty-two. His relics were on this day translated to Compostella, in Spain, where they are held in great veneration, people resorting thither from all parts of Christendom, to pay their pious devotions and fulfil their vows.

26.—St. Ann, mother of the B. Virgin Mary.

AUGUST.

6th.—*Our Lord's Transfiguration*, when he appeared in glory on Mount Tabor, between Moses and Elias, in presence of his three apostles, Peter, James, and John. Matt. xvii.

10.—St. Lawrence, deacon to Pope Xystus II. was broiled on a gridiron for the faith of Christ ; which cruel martyrdom he suffered with incomparable fortitude and patience, in the year two hundred and fifty-three.

142 THE CATHOLIC SCHOOL BOOK.

15th.—*Assumption of the B. V. Mary,* a feast in memory of her being taken into heaven, both body and soul, after her dissolution; which by a constant tradition in the church, has ever been piously believed to have happened in the year thirty-six.

24.—St. Bartholomew, the apostle, having preached the gospel in India, and passing thence into the greater Armenia after he had converted innumerable people to the faith, was barbarously flayed alive by command of King Astages, and then beheaded, in the year forty-four.

SEPTEMBER.

8th.—*The Feast of her Nativity,* of whom the Author of all life and salvation was born to the world.

11th.—*The Exaltation of the Holy Cross;* when Heraclitus brought it back in triumph to Jerusalem, in the year six hundred and twenty-eight.

31st.—St. Matthew, apostle and evangelist, after preaching the gospel in Ethiopia, was slain at the altar as he celebrated the divine mysteries, in the year forty-four.

29th.—*Michaelmas,* a festival instituted in honour of St. Michael the archangel and of the nine orders of holy angels; to commend the whole Church of God to their patronage, by whose charitable ministry we daily receive from God, as the original source, such innumerable benefits. It is called the dedication of St. Michael, from the dedicating of a church to him in Rome by Pope Boniface III, in the year six hundred and eight.

OCTOBER.

18th.—St. Luke, the evangelist, who filled with the Holy Ghost after he had endured many afflictions for the name of Christ, died in Bythnia, in the year seventy-four. His sacred bones were brought to Constantinople, and thence translated to Padua.

28th.—SS. Simon, the Cananite, and Jude, otherwise called Thaddeus. The first preached the gospel in Egypt, the latter in Mesopotamia, and afterwards going together into Persia, after having converted an infinite number of that nation to the faith, they accomplished their martyrdom in the year sixty-eight.

NOVEMBER

1st.—*All Saints,* a solemnity in memory of all the Saints; since the whole year is too short to afford a separate feast for each of them.

2nd.—*All Souls,* a day appointed by the Church for the living to offer up their prayers and suffrages for the repose of the faithful departed.

30th.—St. Andrew, apostle, having preached the gospel in

Thrace and Scythia, he was apprehended by Egeas the Procon-sul; he was first imprisoned, then most cruelly beaten, and last-ly fastened to a cross, where he lived two days, preaching to the people; and having besought our Lord not to permit him to be taken down, encompassed with a great light from Heaven, he gave up his blessed soul, at Patras in Achaia, in the year sixty-nine.

DECEMBER.

8th.—*Conception of the glorious and ever B. V. Mary,* Mother of God; a feast instituted by St. Anselm, Archbishop of Canter-bury, in the year one thousand and seventy, and commanded af-terwards by Sextus IV. to be generally observed, in the year fourteen hundred and forty-six.

21st.—St. Thomas, apostle; having preached the gospel to the Parthians, Medes, Persians, and Hyreans, he went into India, where he instructed the people in the Christian faith; for which, by the King's command, he was pierced through the body with lances, and gave up his blessed soul at Ca'amina, in the year forty-four.

25th—*Christ's Nativity,* a solemn festival celebrated annually by the Catholic Church from the time of the Apostles, in com-memoration of our Saviour's birth at Bethlehem, called Christmas from the mass then celebrated in honour of his holy birth. The nativity of our Lord is a great subject of joy to Christians: all ought to participate in the joy which the angels declared to the shepherds. Christ being born for the salvation of all. This joy consists in giving glory to God and in relishing the peace given to men of good will. The faithful ought to give great atten-tion to this adorable mystery. They ought not to fail to re-ceive the most holy sacrament; they ought to go to church, as the shepherds went to Bethlehem, full of faith, admiration and gladness; beholding the Son of God made man; they ought to adore him, to give him thanks, to learn from the child Jesus, humility, simplicity, a contempt of riches, flying from honours, a retirement from the world, self-denial, the love of sufferings, mortification, penance; they ought to reflect on the excess of charity, wherewith the Eternal Father hath loved us, having given to us his only Son, to deliver us from sin; and, by such a re-flexion, to excite themselves to love God with their whole heart, and most earnestly to hate sin.

26.—St. Stephen, the first martyr after Christ's ascension, was stoned to death by the Jews, in the year thirty-four.

17.—St. John, apostle and evangelist; after writing his gospel, his banishment, and receiving his Revelations, lived to the time of Trajan the emperor, and both founded and governed the

Churches of Asia. Finally, worn out with old age, he died at Ephesus, aged ninety-three, in the year sixty-eight, and was buried near the same city.

28th.—*Holy Innocents*, a feast in commemoration of the infants barbarously slaughtered by Herod, when he sought to take away the life of our blessed Saviour. It is also called Childer-Mass Day, from the particular commemoration of those martyred children in the Mass of that day.

19th.—St. Thomas, archbishop of Canterbury, and patron of the English clergy, for maintaining the privileges of the Church of God, was martyred at Vespers in his own cathedral, in the year one thousand one hundred and seventy.

The several festivals of the saints are instituted by the Church to honour God in his saints, to teach us to imitate their virtues, and honour their martyrdom and sufferings for the faith of Christ.

NECESSARY RULES FOR A CHRISTIAN.

Often examine your thoughts, words, and actions, especially after much business, conversation, etc., that you may discern and amend your faults.

Hold your peace in such things as relate not to you, and where your speech is not for the honour of God, and good of your neighbour.

Often call to mind your past life, and what our Saviour suffered for you in every moment of his.

Live as if you had nothing, and yet possessed all things ; and remember that meat, drink, and clothes, are not the riches of a Christian.

Offer yourself entirely to God; and though you have nothing to return for his favours but yourself, you will be comforted when you consider, that *He gives all that gives himself.* The apostles quitted their poor boats and nets, and received for them a most ample reward. The poor widow gave only two mites, and her offering was preferred before those of the richest.

He easily parts with all things, who considers that he must die and be separated from them.

Use no extravagant or unusual gestures in open assemblies, but on all occasions observe a becoming modesty and discretion.

In all occurences of life, prefer that which conduce the most to the service of God : as to comfort the afflicted, reconcile such as are at variance, visit the sick and imprisoned, and relieve the poor.

Never go to rest at night with any disquiet or trouble on your mind, but endeavour to pacify your conscience by an act of contrition, or by confession, if necessary.

Often confess your sins, and make frequent acts of contrition, aspiration, or ejaculatory prayers, so that you may prevent the deceits of the Devil, conquer temptation, avoid sin, and live under the continual protection of God.

PRAYERS TO BE USED ON DIFFERENT OCCASIONS.

A PRAYER WHEN WE ENTER INTO THE CHURCH.

How awful is this place! this is the house of God, and the gate of Heaven; vouchsafe to purify me, O Lord, and grant that I may here think of nothing but of Thee.

A PRAYER AT GOING OUT OF THE CHURCH.

Happy are they, O Lord, who always dwell in thy house, and who are employed in nothing but in praising thee. I am going where I believe thy providence carries me; in every place I shall always find Theo present.

A PRAYER BEFORE SPIRITUAL READING.

Happy is the man who is well instructed in thy holy law, O my God. Give me the spirit of understanding, the docility that is necessary, and an ardent charity for putting in execution what thou shalt make me know to be acceptable to thee.

A PRAYER AFTER SPIRITUAL READING.

Make me love the truth which thou hast made known to me, O my God, and grant me the grace to practice what I know to be according to thy holy will.

A PRAYER BEFORE VISITS AND CONVERSATIONS.

Seeing that my tongue is to celebrate Thy praises for all eternity, O my God, permit me not to offend Thee in this visit and conversation.

A PRAYER AFTER VISITINGS AND CONVERSATIONS.

Vouchsafe to pardon, O Lord, all the faults committed in this entertainment, and permit not my words ever to be a scandal or offence to any one.

G

A PRAYER BEFORE GOING OUT OF THE HOUSE.

Vouchsafe, O Lord, to direct me in thy way of justice and truth, and remove far from me all occasions of sin.

A PRAYER AFTER RETURNING HOME.

I give Thee infinite thanks, O my God, for having preserved me from so many dangers; and I beg of thy infinite mercy to bring me at last to Thy heavenly country.

A PRAYER WHEN WE BEGIN ANY WORK.

I offer unto Thee, O Lord, this my work, and beg of Thee to be the director of it, as I hope Thou wilt be the reward thereof.

A PRAYER AT THE END OF WORK.

I give Thee thanks, O Lord, for the blessing given to my work, and I beg of Thee to accept of it in satisfaction for my sins.

GRACE BEFORE EATING.

Bless to us, O Lord, all these thy gifts, which we are about to receive of thy bounty : through Jesus Christ our Lord. Amen.

GRACE AFTER EATING.

We give thanks, Almighty God, for all thy benefits; who livest and reignest world without end. Amen.

ANOTHER PRAYER.

Vouchsafe, O Lord, to nourish my soul, as Thou hast fed my body ; and grant that after temporal nourishment I may have eternal life. Amen.

THE CHRISTIAN DOCTRINE.

THE LORD'S PRAYER.

Our Father who art in Heaven, hallowed be Thy name; Thy kingdom come; Thy will be done on earth as it is in Heaven; give us this day our daily bread; and forgive us our trespasses, as we forgive them that trespass against us; and lead us not into temptation; but deliver us from evil. Amen.

THE ANGELIC SALUTATION.

Hail Mary, full of grace, our Lord is with thee. Blessed art thou amongst women! and blessed is the fruit of thy womb, JESUS. Holy Mary, Mother of God, pray for us sinners, now, and at the hour of our death. Amen.

THE APOSTLES' CREED.

I believe in God, the Father Almighty, Creator of Heaven and Earth; and in Jesus Christ, his only son, our Lord, who was conceived by the Holy Ghost, born of the Virgin Mary; suffered under Pontius Pilate, was crucified, dead and buried; he descended into Hell; the third day he rose again from the dead; he ascended into Heaven; sitteth at the right hand of God, the Father Almighty; from thence he shall come to judge the living and the dead. I believe in the Holy Ghost, the holy Catholic Church, the communion of saints, the forgiveness of sins, the resurrection of the body, and life everlasting. Amen.

THE TEN COMMANDMENTS.

I am the Lord thy Lord, who brought thee out of the land of Egypt, and out of the house of bondage.

1. Thou shalt not have strange gods before me. Thou shalt not make to thyself any graven thing, nor any similitude that is in Heaven above, or in the Earth below, or of things that are in the water under the Earth; thou shalt not adore nor worship them. I am the Lord thy God, strong and jealous, visiting the sins of the fathers upon their children to the third and fourth generation of them that hate me, and showing mercy to thousands of those that love me and keep my commandments.

II. Thou shalt not take the name of the Lord thy God in vain; for the Lord will not hold him guiltless that takes the name of the Lord his God in vain.

III. Remember thou keep holy the Sabbath day. Six days shalt thou labour and do all thy work; but the seventh is the Sabbath of the Lord thy God. On it thou shalt do no work, neither thou, nor thy son, nor thy daughter, nor thy man-servant, nor thy maid-servant, nor thy cattle, nor the stranger which is within thy gates. For in six days the Lord made Heaven and Earth, and the sea, and all that are in them, and rested on the seventh day; therefore hath the Lord blessed the Sabbath-day, and sanctified it.

IV. Honour thy father and mother, that thy days may be long in the land which the Lord thy God shall give thee.

V. Thou shalt not kill.

VI. Thou shalt not commit adultery.

VII. Thou shalt not steal.

VIII. Thou shalt not bear false witness against thy neighbour.

IX. Thou shalt not covet thy neighbour's wife.

X. Thou shalt not covet thy neighbour's goods, nor his man-servant, nor his maid-servant, nor his ox, nor his ass, nor anything that is his.

THE SEVEN SACRAMENTS.

1. Baptism, Matt. xxviii. 19.   2. Confirmation.   Acts vii. 17.
2. Eucharist, Matt. xxvi. 26.   4. Penance, John xx. 23.   5. Extreme Unction, James v. 14.   6. Holy Orders, Matt. xxvi.   7. Matrimony, Matt. xix. 6.

THE THREE THEOLOGICAL VIRTUES.

1. Faith   2. Hope.   3. Charity.

THE FOUR CARDINAL VIRTUES.

1. Prudence.   2. Justice.   3. Fortitude.   4. Temperance.

THE SEVEN GIFTS OF THE HOLY GHOST.

1. Wisdom.   2. Understanding.   3. Counsel.   4. Fortitude.
5. Knowledge.   6. Godliness.   7. The Fear of the Lord.

THE TWELVE FRUITS OF THE HOLY GHOST.

1. Charity.   2. Joy.   3. Peace.   4. Patience.   5. Benignity.

6. Goodness.   7. Longanimity.   8. Mildness.   9. Faith. 10.
Modesty.   11. Continence. 12. Charity.

TWO PRECEPTS OF CHARITY.

1. Thou shalt love the Lord thy God with thy whole heart
with thy whole soul, with all thy strength, and with all thy mind,
2. And thy neighbour as thyself.

PRECEIPTS OF THE CHURCH.

1. To keep certain appointed days holy, which obligation consists chiefly in hearing Mass, and resting from servile works.
2. To observe the commanded days of fast and abstinence.
3. To contribute to the support of your pastor.
4. To confess your sins to your pastor, at least once a year.
5. To receive the blessed sacrament at least once a year; and
that about Easter.
5. Not to solemnize marriage at certain times, nor within certain degrees of kindred, nor privately, without witnesses.

THE CORPORAL WORKS OF MERCY.

1. To feed the hungry. 2. To give drink to the thirsty. 3.
To clothe the naked. 4. To visit and ransom captives. 5. To
harbour the harbourless. 6. To visit the sick. 7. To bury the
dead.

THE EIGHT BEATITUDES.

1. Blessed are the poor in spirit, for theirs is the kingdom of
Heaven.
2. Blessed are they that mourn : for they shall be comforted.
3. Blessed are the meek, for they shall possess the land.
4. Blessed are they who hunger and thirst after justice, for they
shall be filled.
5. Blessed are the merciful, for they shall find mercy.
6. Blessed are the clean of heart, for they shall see God.

7. Blessed are the peace-makers, for they shall be called the sons of God.

8. Blessed are they who suffer persecution for justice's sake, for theirs is the kingdom of Heaven.

O⁧ SIN.

SIN is two-fold; original an actual. Actual is divided into mortal and venial.

THE CAPITAL SEVEN SINS, COMMONLY CALLED MORTAL OR DEADLY SINS.

	Contrary Virtues.	
Pride,		Humility,
Covetousness,		Liberality,
Lust,		Chastity,
Wrath,		Meekness,
Gluttony,		Temperance,
Envy,		Brotherly-love,
Sloth,		Diligence.

Six Sins against the Holy Ghost.

1. Despair of salvation. 2. Presumption of God's mercy. 3. Impugning the known truth. 4. Envy at another's spiritual good. 5. Obstinacy in sin. 6. Final importance.

Things necessary for a Penitent Sinner.

Contrition of heart. Entire confession to an approved priest. Satisfaction by works.

Contrition consists in a hearty displeasure at sin past, for the love of God, and a firm resolution not to sin any more.

Four Sins crying to Heaven for Vengeance.

1. Wilful murder. 2. Sodomy. 3. Oppression of the poor. 4. Defrauding labourers of their wages.

Nine ways of being accessory to another person's sins.

1. By counsel. 2. By command. 3. By consent. 4. By pro-vocation. 5. By praise or flattery. 6. By concealment. 7. By partaking. 7. By silence. 8. By defence of the ill done.

Three Eminent Good Works.

1. Alms-deeds, or works of mercy.   2. Prayer.   3. Fasting.

Three Evangelical Counsels.

1. Voluntary poverty.   2. Perpetual charity.   3. Entire ˉobe-
dience.

The Four Last Things to be Remembered.

1. Death.   2. Judgment.   3. Hell.   4. Heaven.

APPROBATION.

We have seen and approved the book called THE CATHOLIC SCHOOL BOOK, and we recommend the use of it in our Diocese.

　　　　　　　　　　　　　† IG. *Bishop of Montreal.*

Montreal, the 1st of July, 1843.

　　　　　　　　　　BALTIMORE, *8th July*, 1824.

THE CATHOLIC SCHOOL BOOK is, in my judgment, an elementary work of singular merit. I will rejoice to see it introduced into all the Catholic Schools in this country.

　　　　　　　　　　　AMB. *Archbp. Balt.*

　　　　　　　　　NEW-YORK, 1st *Sept.* 1824.

I have read the CATHOLIC SCHOOL BOOK, and believe it to be well adapted to the understanding of youth, and calculated to give them early ideas of morality and virtue. I therefore recommend its adoption to our Schools, to the Clergy and laity of this Diocese.

　　　　　　　　　JOHN CONNOLLY,
　　　　　　　　　R. C. Bishop of New-York.

Sir,—Having looked over your CATHOLIC SCHOOL BOOK, I think it right to tell you, that in my opinion, it is far the most complete work of its kind in our language, and eminently entitled to the patronage of the Catholic public. What I particularly admire in it is, that, instead of those trifling, and in some instances irreligious stories to be found in books of the same nature, it contains a series of Moral Lessons and Scripture History, proper for the instruction and adapted to the understanding and abilities of children, who are learning to read. As such, I shall not fail to recommend it in those places of education over which I have any authority or influence.

　　　　　I am, Sir,
　　　　　　　Your faithful servant,

　　　　　　　　　J. MILNER, D.D.

Mr. W. E. Andrews.